COURT OF SERPENTS AND SECRETS

THE SHADOW BOUND QUEEN

ELIZA RAINE

ELIZA RAINE

COURT OF SERPENTS AND SECRETS

THE SHADOW BOUND QUEEN

A BRIDES OF FAE AND MIST NOVEL

For everyone who never gives up.
For the love of Odin, you've got this.

CHAPTER 1
REYNA

Mazrith and I stared at each other, neither breaking the deafening silence. My hands shook as his presence seemed to swell and harden, becoming more than a little terrifying.

The rage-filled roar he had made in the vision rang in my ears. His mother's blood spilling over his black-and-white mottled skin played over and over in my head.

I had just accused him of killing his mother and being a gold-fae, and he was staring at me with hatred in his eyes, every inch the fierce and deadly Prince of the Shadow Court.

"Say something," I whispered eventually, forcing the words to leave my lips.

"You wish me to deny it?" His voice was a hiss, and the fury drained from his eyes, replaced with a look so cold I couldn't hold his gaze.

I had no idea what I wanted him to say.

I already knew it was true.

Rubbing my hands over my face, I tried to put the pieces together, tried to make sense of what I had seen. "How do you have shadow magic if you are not a shadow-fae?" The first vision I'd had of him swam back to me. His mother had said he would have enough magic for five years. But Mazrith had been a famously powerful shadow-fae long before his mother died.

And why had he ended her life?

"I am not a gold-fae," Mazrith spat.

"Then what are you?"

"Nothing *Yggdrasil* has seen before, or ever wishes to," he snapped, and turned away from me. "We need to leave."

"What? No, we need to talk! Mazrith, you have to tell me what I just saw."

"I *have* to tell you nothing."

Anger coursed through me and I dropped my hands, slapping one hard against my thigh. The sharp sound made him turn back to me. "I told you everything," I snarled through gritted teeth. "*Everything*. Secrets and fears I have admitted to no one."

He took a step toward me so fast I gasped, only stopping when he was towering over me. His skin was perfect, his sharp cheekbones, straight nose and pointed ears exactly as a beautiful fae Prince should be. I could see no trace of the mottled, scarred, mess of flesh I'd seen in the vision.

Was it under there? Now? Hidden by magic? I

2

reached up to touch his face, but he spoke, and the icy steel in his voice made me freeze.

"I killed my mother."

My heart hammered in my chest, and I lowered my hand.

He continued to glare down at me, tense as rock. "I am not a gold-fae and I am not a shadow-fae."

"But—"

"That is as much as you will learn until we are out of the sacred tree and away from my warriors."

I started to speak but stopped. Shadows were tumbling across his irises and around his staff. He had said earlier that being inside the tree of *Yggdrasil* too long made fae wild. And the others were just the other side of the waterfall.

Maybe he was right. This wasn't the time to talk.

Hands still shaking, I squared my shoulders. "Fine, but you must promise—"

"I promise nothing. Hold your breath."

I gave a cry of alarm, then gulped a desperate breath as he grabbed my hand and stepped off the disc into the water.

He swam powerfully hard, dragging us both through the current much faster than when we had come through the first time, but the disorientation was no less unsettling. Panic and anger consumed me as I was pulled through the water.

As soon as we surfaced on the other side, I yanked my

hand back to smack his shoulder, kicking my legs frantically as I immediately started to sink.

"You stupid, childish, selfish *veslingr*!" I yelled at him, as he wrapped an arm around my waist and started to propel us back to the boat. "I'd agreed to stop asking you questions, you didn't need to try to drown me, you immature, selfish—"

"You already said that one," I heard Frima say, before strong hands pulled me up onto the deck of the boat.

I glowered at Mazrith pulling himself onto the deck. He wouldn't meet my eyes.

"Well, he deserves selfish twice," I snapped, still panting and shaking with shock.

I may have agreed to pause my questions, but the images were still coursing through my head, adrenaline and confusion still raging through me.

I needed time to work out what I had just seen, but he had deliberately given me none.

Why? Had he just dragged me through the water like that as punishment for seeing something I shouldn't have? Or was he genuinely desperate to get out of the tree of *Yggdrasil*?

It was difficult to take my eyes from him as I dried myself, and when Voror swooped down onto the deck I was relieved to have a distraction from the hulking mass of cold anger.

"I lost your feather," I told the owl.

With a baleful look, Voror turned his head to an

impossible angle, then plucked one with his beak before fluttering over to me with it.

"Thanks, and sorry," I said, tucking into my headband.

"I will be naked by the time you are done," he muttered into my mind. "I see your quest was successful, though."

"What?"

The owl blinked slowly at me. "Every time I think you may be smarter that I credited you, I am forced to re-evaluate." I glared at him. "You were trying to reveal the staircase. You have succeeded."

"We have?"

Voror gave a mental sigh, then took off, flying to a part of the trunk opposite the statue of Thor. There, barely visible against the wood behind it, was indeed a staircase. It zigzagged its way up the inside of the trunk, disappearing into the high canopies of foliage that covered the wood as it rose. The owl landed neatly on the carved railing and blinked in our direction.

"Is that what caused all that noise?" asked Svangrior, standing at the edge of the boat. His eyes were flitting over everything in his view and he was almost as tense and on-edge as Mazrith. "I thought I'd imagined it."

Tait was staring in excitement. "Oh no, this is real. I knew the rumors were true." He clapped his hands together. "The secrets of this world will never end!"

Mazrith moved past him and shadows flowed from

his staff into the sail of the boat, floating us toward the staircase.

He still hadn't looked at me.

Gripping the railing, I gritted my teeth and closed my eyes. I needed to shift the image of him—mottle-skinned with his hand around the dagger sunk into his mother's chest—from my mind. At least for now.

He would not speak of it here, no matter how much I burned to know what would have led him to end his own mother's life. Whatever had happened, there *must* have been a reason. He had loved her, he had made that clear many times before, and so had his friends.

The black, soulless eyes and puckered, rotting wounds flashed into my mind, along with the tiniest flicker of doubt.

I took a breath and let go of the railing, opening my eyes.

I trusted Mazrith. To my own surprise, I *respected* him. He was *not* a cold-blooded murderer. I knew that for certain. I wouldn't have been able to kiss him the way I had, embrace his touch, let him take me to such a place of pleasure, *of vulnerability*, if I had believed for a moment he was truly a monster.

He would tell me what had happened, to him *and* his mother, and there would be an explanation that made sense. There had to be.

CHAPTER 2

REYNA

I t only took the boat minutes to reach the staircase, and up close it was just as intricately carved and beautiful as the glimpse from my vision had shown it to be. Winding vines and leaves had been molded from the wood to create a high railing all the way up, and I could easily believe it was the work of the tree itself rather than a craftsperson, it was so organic and natural.

"Everyone, wait here," Mazrith barked when Frima used her shadows to anchor the boat to the staircase.

"Really?" Uncharacteristic annoyance layered Frima's words, sharper than her usual clipped sarcasm. "What is the point in being one of the strongest warriors in *Yggdrasil* if all I do is babysit and wait for you to do shit?"

Mazrith whirled at her words, and she hastily backed up a step. "I told you to wait here, and you shall do as you are bid." Solid steel laced his words, and she nodded once.

"Yes, Maz. Of course."

"You, come with me." His order was clearly for me. Even though he still hadn't looked at me, his shadows swirled around my legs, nudging me toward the edge of the deck. Apprehensively, I let them lead me and then steady me, as I moved carefully from the boat onto the staircase. Mazrith's hulking form filled the space behind me, and I began to climb.

My thighs were burning by the time we reached the top of the zigzagging staircase. In fact, it wasn't the top, it was just the first ledge we had come to that was accessible, carved into the wood of the trunk of *Yggdrasil* and peppered with foliage. Small bushes of purple flowers dotted the earthy ledge, and pretty orange daisies hung on winding vines.

I recognized what I saw at the end of it. A large iron-bound chest, identical to the one from the vision of Mazrith's father.

Please, please let him have stashed Thor's Talisman here, I prayed as I stepped off the staircase and onto the platform.

"I told you there would be something to find here," Voror said, landing on the staircase railing. "And I am rarely wrong." The smugness we would have to endure from the haughty owl if the amulet was indeed in the chest would be insufferable. But worth it.

Snaking green vines had wrapped themselves all over the box, and I wondered how long ago the King had been there.

I reached out to pull them away from the chest lid and pain zipped up my arm. Before I could even cry out, I couldn't breathe. My lungs had just... stopped working.

I clutched at my chest, trying to make a sound, before falling onto my backside, blind panic taking me. Mazrith's shadows rushed me, and panic flooded my body as they moved toward my mouth, then into my throat.

With a short burst of pain, the pressure on my lungs vanished, and I was able to breathe again. The shadows left as quickly as they had entered and I choked down air, my fingers wrapped around my throat, hands sweating.

"What the fates just happened?" I gasped, blinking tears from my eyes as Mazrith moved beside me and dropped into a crouch.

He made no move to touch me, and still didn't meet my eyes, but I was sure I could see concern mingled with the fury on his face. At least, I *wanted* to see concern. "A trap," he growled. "One of my father's favorites. I should have guessed."

I took a few deep, heaving breaths, and once my breathing had settled, Mazrith's shadows moved to the box. As they flurried around it, all the vines recoiled. There was a loud snap and the lid creaked open.

Letting go of my throat, I tipped forward onto my knees to look into the chest.

The most beautiful axe I had ever seen glinted back up at me. It was made from silver metal and set along both blades were the largest collection of gemstones I had ever seen. Intricate winding vines were etched into both blades, so similar to the carvings in the staircase railings that I wondered if the axe was connected to the tree of life.

"It's incredible," I breathed.

"It is stolen," Mazrith rumbled. "That did not belong to my father." Almost reluctantly, he pulled it from the chest. I heard metal moving and looked again. Bags and bags of coins lined the bottom of the box, along with a handful of other smaller items. A scroll of paper, a small iron box, a bracelet of intensely red rubies, and...

"Is that it? Is that Thor's Talisman?"

Mazrith reached for the hammer-shaped amulet and let out a long breath as his fingers closed around the metal. "Yes."

"Oh, thank the gods." I dropped back onto my backside, relief coursing through me.

"This is a wolf claw," Mazrith muttered. He had opened the smaller box, a single damaged, yellowing claw inside.

"Strange thing to lock away where nobody can find it."

Mazrith didn't respond, just snapped the box shut. He began pulling everything from the chest, loading it all into the pouches on his belt and the pockets in his cloak. He passed me two bags of coins and the ruby bracelet to put in my own pockets and I blinked down at the treasure.

This would have been enough to buy me a lifetime of freedom.

But what kind of freedom would it have been? A life on the run. *A life alone.*

"That is everything. We must leave." Mazrith stood and straightened, his staff in one hand and the magnificent axe in the other.

I stared up at him, awe washing over me. "You look like a king, holding that," I said.

Darkness swamped his eyes, his mouth tightening as he glanced at me, then looked away again.

Definitely not the right thing to say.

He swept past me and down the stairs. Slowly, I got to my feet and followed.

The tension in Frima and Svangrior leaked away almost as soon as we had left the tree and were on the root-river back to the Shadow Court. Frustratingly, the same was not true of Mazrith. He stood rod-straight and glowering at the prow, glaring out at the river around us for a short while, then locked himself in his cabin, commanding Frima to guide us the rest of the way back.

After an hour of my thoughts tumbling about incoherently, I knocked on his door. "Mazrith?"

There was no answer.

Frima came over as I leaned against the closed door with a sigh. "You should get some sleep. It's another eight hours back and it's been an infernally long day."

"I don't know if I *can* sleep."

She glanced at the door, then at me. "I'm sure you'll sort it out. Whatever the fates it is that you two are neck-deep in."

"I hope so. He's not exactly being forthcoming right now. In fact, he's refusing to talk to me at all. It's..." I tried to pick a word. Infuriating? Impossible? *Terrifying*. "Annoying."

Frima snorted. "I don't remember you being particularly *forthcoming* either." She tilted her head. "You two are the strangest pair."

"You're telling me," I muttered, then pressed my forehead to the wood. The image of him from my vision forced its way into my head.

He had been hiding that secret his whole life, never sharing it with anyone. The burden his alone. Had he been born like that? Did somebody or something turn him into that?

I let out yet another sigh, wishing he would talk to me. Wishing he would let me soothe some of that awful, rigid tension from him.

"Sleep well, Maz," I muttered. "And I will try to do the same."

CHAPTER 3

REYNA

I did sleep, but not well. Somewhat unsurprisingly, my dreams were filled with him. Not of his earth-shattering touches of pleasure, as I would have liked to dream of him, but of his puckered, scarred skin and black eyes. I dreamed of him on his stepmother's throne, doing all the things she had done, and licking the blood of his victims off his own chalk-white lips. I dreamed of him standing next to the Elder as she sang, the scars on his face opening, blackening, leaking golden liquid over his disintegrating body.

When I woke, I was drenched in sweat. Brynja was bustling around at the foot of the bed, folding things from the chests into large sacks.

"My Lady?" She straightened when I sat up too fast and groaned. "We are nearly at the shore. Would you like tea?"

"No, thank you," I said thickly. "Some water would be good though, please."

I dressed quickly in my work clothes and found myself relieved to see the twinkling gloom of the Shadow Court when I went out on deck just as the boat slid onto the dark sand with a gentle thud.

"Who'd have thought I'd ever be happy to be back here?" I muttered to myself as I moved to where Tait was standing, clutching the sphere from the Ice Court game. "Where's Mazrith?" I asked him.

Before the shadow-spinner could answer, the Prince swept past me.

"Mazrith—" I started, but he gripped the wood and vaulted over the railing, his dark furs disappearing after him. I sighed and clenched my teeth. "Never mind."

Frima walked past me, three huge sacks thrown over her shoulders. "Come on."

The open-sided cart that had brought us down the mountain was waiting for us, but Mazrith was nowhere to be seen when my feet found the sand. Voror swooped overhead, and his voice sounded in my mind.

"The stupid bear and the Prince have left."

"Left?"

"Yes. The stupid bear—"

"*Arthur*. The bear who saved my life," I corrected him, rolling my eyes and giving Frima a smile as she frowned at me.

"Fine. Arthur, the stupid bear, was waiting for him when we arrived."

I turned to Frima as the cart began to move through the forest. "Do you know where Mazrith has gone?"

"No. Your owl just told you he met with Arthur?" she guessed.

"Yes."

She shrugged. "I'm sure he'll make it back to the palace before we will."

When we entered the Serpent Suites though, there was no sign of Mazrith. Kara, however, was sitting in the big chair by the fire, and she dropped her book and launched herself at me before I was even fully in the room. Svangrior tutted and marched through to the war room, and Frima smiled, dropped her bags, then left the Suites.

"Reyna! You're back safe!" Kara squeezed me hard, and I squeezed her back.

"I am. Where's Lhoris?" The big man lumbered through the door as I spoke, his bearded cheeks splitting in a smile when he saw me.

"You are safe," he said.

"Only just," I said, with a rueful smile. I felt a jolt of shame that I couldn't show them another braid, but their obvious delight at seeing me in one piece forced it away.

"Tell us everything," Kara said, pulling me to the fire.

"I will, but first I need to make sure Voror is here. He needs to hear all of this too." I looked up pointedly at the rafters.

"He wasn't with you?"

"No, the Ice Court is too cold for him. He stayed inside *Yggdrasil*. Voror?"

There was a fluttering of white, then the owl soared down, landing on the back of the armchair.

I told them all everything that had happened since I left, omitting the swimming lesson details, and what had happened in the tree on the way back. Voror already knew most of that part, and my friends couldn't find out about our quest for the mist-staff.

Kara was typically wide-eyed when I was finished. "Orm saved you?" She shook her head. "There is a secret game being played, Reyna. You must be careful."

"I am being careful. But I don't think it was for any reason other than Orm wishes a worse fate for me and Mazrith than being crushed by ice. He's just cruel, and twisted."

"I wish he had not recovered from Lady Kaldar's attack under the water," muttered Lhoris.

"You and me both. But sadly he did."

"Do you trust Dakkar?" Lhoris's eyes darkened.

"Not trust, no. But I can't help liking him and his family."

"Hmm."

"The other strange thing," I said, glancing around the room to ensure it was empty, before turning back to Kara. "Is that I didn't have any visions through other people's eyes while I was there."

Somehow, her eyes widened even further. "That *is* interesting," she said.

"Did you learn anything in the library while I was away?"

"Sort of. Well, I learned lots about magic."

"Anything that could explain how someone might be giving me access to their magic? Perhaps someone who wasn't in the Ice Court with us?"

Kara shook her head. "Fae with strong mind-magic — usually shadow-fae — could make you see things in your head, or even feel things, but they can't give you access to other people's heads. And fae can't give other people use of their magic."

Mazrith's mom's words floated through my mind. *I can give you enough magic for five years.* "Are you sure about that?"

Kara gave me a look. "Unless you killed a fae in such an honorable manner that they opted to give you their magic with their dying breath, then yes. I am sure nobody has given you their magic."

I stared at her. "Say that again."

She frowned. "I read that the only way magic can be passed between beings is voluntarily, and to the person who ended your life. It was the god's way of recognizing valor in battle. If you respected the person who killed you enough, you could make them stronger. But, if you were killed in an underhanded way, your murderer wouldn't get your power. It's a little defunct in today's world, where the only beings with power have no honor, but I suppose it made sense in ancient times."

The parts clicked into place in my head.

The only way Mazrith's mother could give him her magic was if *he* killed her.

She *did* sacrifice herself for him.

My heart hurt as I remembered his bellow of rage and pain. More than anything, I wanted to go to him, and I was halfway to my feet before I remembered that I had no idea where he was.

"Reyna, are you okay?"

"Yes." I blinked at her, sitting back down. "I'm sorry, that... that makes something else make sense."

"What?"

I shook my head and looked at her apologetically. "I can't say."

Kara shrugged. "Okay. Then returning to your visions, what was different in the Ice Court that might have affected them?"

"I was not with you in the Ice Court," said Voror.

I turned to the owl, dragging my focus back. "Are you saying that you are giving me the visions? Or the power to have visions?"

"If I am, then I am not aware of it. But I was not with you. It may be relevant."

I relayed his words to Kara. "It's possible, I guess." After a few moments thought she said, "I did find out about other magical beings that aren't fae, like you asked."

"And are any of them seem like something..." I cast about for the correct words. "*I* could be?" It didn't sound right, but I didn't know how else to ask.

She gave me an apologetic look. "Not really, no. Few of them were humanoid, and the ones that were were either wolves, four feet tall, or made of light."

"Oh."

"If you have magic, then..." My gut tightened, and Lhoris took a long breath. "I hate to say it, Reyna, but you're probably a fae."

"No. I'm not fae. I can't be." *Could I?*

"Reyna, without knowing who your parents are, you have no way of knowing what you might be." I had expected the words from Kara, but it was Lhoris who had spoken them.

I looked at him in surprise, unease trickling through my veins.

Lhoris hated the fae. They took him from his clan, beat him, and kept him prisoner. I had only ever heard fury and loathing from him whenever their kind were mentioned, for more than a decade.

But there was no anger or hatred in his eyes when he looked at me. They were filled with compassion. "I knew the first time you told me what you had seen after working with gold that you were different."

I stared at him. "But... fae?"

"You are using some kind of magic. There is little point denying it. But that does not make you a different person from the one I have loved and cared for the last fifteen years."

Emotion made my skin tight and my stomach lurch. Without hesitation, I leaned forward, wrapping my arms around the big man. "You wouldn't hate me if I was fae?" I murmured into his thick hair.

"Nothing in the world would make me hate you, Reyna."

I sucked in a shaky breath.

A loud bang made me pull away from him.

I turned in Lhoris's stiffening arms. Kara seemed to shrink a little.

The bang was Prince Mazrith opening the door to his suites. And he was finally looking at me.

CHAPTER 4

REYNA

"Reyna, I need you to come with me." His barked, emotionless words rang through the room.

"I'm speaking with my friends," I said coolly, trying to fill my head with the version of him I had been with in the pool, in the glacier. That version of Mazrith might even have said hello to my friends. This version... This version was the one who had kidnapped me in the first place. The hard, hulking, angry warrior.

"That can wait. We are leaving." He turned and strode from the room, leaving the door open behind him.

I ground my teeth. "I'll see you in... a few hours, I hope." I gave Lhoris a kiss on the cheek. "Thank you." He smiled.

"Where are you going?" Kara whispered, still looking at the open door.

"More secret quests," I said with a shrug and a smile. "But not far. And I don't think anywhere dangerous."

"Be careful all the same," she said with a quick hug.

Mazrith was standing, rigid, in the corridor. He began to walk as soon as he saw me and I hurried to catch up to him.

"We're going to *Ravensstar*, I assume?"

"Do not speak of it here."

I couldn't help my face screwing up in annoyance. "Are we to speak of anything at all?"

"If we are, it will not be here."

"That's getting familiar," I muttered, but fell silent.

By the time we reached the top of the stairs to the bridge between the towers, I was so out of breath that I couldn't have spoken if I'd wanted to.

The beauty of the Court beyond the towers was incredible enough to make me pause when we walked out onto the bridge. I had found myself pleased when the ship returned to the Shadow Court, I thought, staring out over the navy blanket of sparkling pin-pricks.

Could this ever be my home?

I looked to Mazrith, the bubble of hope sinking in my stomach. The last time we had been on this bridge he had told me more of his past than ever before. This time, all I was presented with was his fur-clad back as he strode ahead.

When I caught up to him, he was pressing the Thor amulet to the secret little carving of the snake and crown, and muttering something in ancient words I mostly didn't recognize. After a few seconds he put the amulet back over his head. I looked at the carving, then took a hurried step back as the stone making up the bridge began to crack and move.

"Come," Mazrith said, when the sounds had stopped, and the part of the bridge wall where the carving had been was gone completely.

My heart leaped into my throat as he stepped out into thin air.

"Mazrith!" But he was hovering, something invisible taking his weight.

I stared, shaking my head hard. "No. No, I'm not walking over an invisible bridge," I stammered.

"When you are standing on it, it becomes visible. Come. Now."

Without another word of encouragement, he began to walk out toward the collection of stars he had shown me before.

"Mazrith, I am not crossing this Odin-cursed bridge!" I called after him. He paused, then without turning, waved his staff. Shadows flowed from its tip, solidifying into snakes. They rushed toward me, then hovered like handrails at my sides.

He was sending his shadows to help me, instead of coming himself.

He resumed his strides out over the empty sky, and I hissed another curse. "Freya help me, as that hulking fucking oaf won't."

I moved to the hole in the stone. Clutching each side

of the gap, I tentatively dangled one foot out over the side. A blue shimmer formed beneath my boot. I lowered it, cautiously, and when it made contact with something hard, the shimmer intensified, and a large slab of sparkling navy blue appeared.

Sweating, I gathered my courage. I pushed myself out, forcing my other leg on. More blue shimmers appeared and I peeled my rigid fingers from the stone and immediately groped for the shadow snakes on either side of me. They were reassuringly solid, and I took a deep breath as I got my balance.

"Time to go, Reyna. You can do this."

My legs shook, but I lifted the back one and took a step. The shiny blue bridge was wide, which helped, but the space in front of me was utterly empty, the whole palace and mountainside visible below me. Swallowing down nausea and dizziness, I forced my eyes up and on the figure of Mazrith ahead. With endless deep breaths and the gentle forward motion of the shadow snakes, I coaxed my legs into a rhythm. *Left foot, right foot. Left foot, right foot.*

It took an interminably long time, but eventually I was casting my eyes upward and sending a prayer of thanks to Freya that I had reached the sky island of *Ravensstar*.

And my sparkling surroundings were utterly breathtaking.

A church stood before me, the only building on the island. The ground appeared made of the same shimmering blue light as the bridge, covered in blades of grass and glittering white daisies formed from shimmering, sparkling dust.

The church looked more solid, but as I moved my head and it caught the light, I could swear that it was made from nothing but light. It looked like the traditional churches I had seen in the Gold Court, constructed from triangles stacked on top of each other, except that the tiles covering the multiple slanted roofs were made from something pearlescent and shiny instead of gold or slate. It reminded me of snow.

All the pillars and archways were decorated with snakes, in the same organic, flowing, interlocking style of the staircase inside the tree of *Yggdrasil*. Each part of the roof that came to a point had a shining serpent jutting from it, hissing a shimmering beam of starlight.

There was no sound at all, nor smell, but it didn't feel eerie or claustrophobic. It felt calming.

Mazrith bowed his head in the open doorway for a moment, then entered. My mouth hanging open in awe, I followed him, pausing to run my fingers over the exquisite images, carved from the shining, glittering substance. It was cool to touch but it didn't feel like stone. If I was forced to give it a color, I would have said blue, but it shone pale grey, sparkling ivory, ice-bright — it didn't stop shifting in tone and luminosity. The shadows it cast changed too, shifting in strength and shape as the light moved.

The shadow-fae were as much in need of light as the

rest of us, I thought as I stared, transfixed. There was no shadow without light.

My annoyance with Mazrith for letting me cross the bridge alone had abandoned me. "What is it made from?"

"Nobody knows. It is a secret of the royal family, gifted by the gods, and no substance exists anywhere else like it."

"Do you think the other Courts have an equivalent?"

"Yes."

An aisle ran up the middle of the space, benches lining either side. The ceiling stretched high into the triangles, the angles and beams causing more shimmering, shifting shadows to play over the sparkling surfaces.

Tapestries hung on the walls, all spun from shining silver thread which caught the light too, though they didn't have the ethereal quality of the building itself. An altar stood tall at the end the aisle, and above it beams of light all came together to create some sort of chandelier, lines of glittering dust forming whales and dragons and serpents and wolves.

I'd never even imagined a place so beautiful could exist.

Mazrith stopped before a tapestry showing his mother, and I turned away, wishing to give him privacy. My eyes landed on another tapestry, clearly a family tree.

The Shadow Court royal family tree, I confirmed as I leaned closer, tracing names I didn't recognize across the glimmering fabric.

My gaze paused on a name. Erik. But it was not the name that had made me stop, it was the tiny mark beside the name. It was the rune for shadow. The same one etched into the wrist of Tait, and all the other *shadow-spinner*s in the world. A little flutter whispered through my belly and I frowned.

Why would a member of a fae royal family have a rune-marked symbol by his name?

I scanned them all, and found two more, a male and female.

It must mean something else, I decided. After all, the rune for shadow would be important to the shadow-fae beyond marking their staff-makers. But something felt strange about it, and that funny flutter in my stomach continued.

There was a noise behind me, and I turned around to see Mazrith's shadows flowing from his staff, and a table rising behind the altar. There were three large goblets on it and he moved to the one on the right. I followed, reluctantly leaving the tapestry.

The goblet was filled with stones. They were pearly, almost translucent, but when I reached out and picked one up it immediately turned as dark as the sky of the Shadow Court, filled with a thousand tiny stars.

I let out an appreciative breath. "This is a star stone?"

"Yes." He reached out and took one from the goblet.

"It's beautiful." I moved to grudgingly put the stone back and he waved his hand.

"Keep it. It can't hurt to have a spare."

I nodded and put it in my pocket. "Does this seem too easy to you? There are no puzzles to solve or statues to fight. So far, nothing here has tried to kill us."

Mazrith scowled. "There was nothing easy about finding Thor's Talisman. We were incredibly lucky."

I shook my head. "There was no luck involved. Finding the amulet *was* easy, compared to getting the jade — my vision showed us where to find it."

He looked at me, then cast his eyes slowly around the stunning church. His gaze lingered on the family tree tapestry. "Someone must be sending you the visions. Someone who knows our quest and knew the King hid his belongings inside the chest in *Yggdrasil*. It is likely the same person who wrote the inscription in the shrine and sent your owl."

"Do you think both the memory visions *and* the spying visions are being sent to me?"

"Yes."

My conversation with Kara about magic being shared played in my head. "Can visions be 'sent' like that?"

He drew his gaze back to me but didn't hold it long. "No fae could be sending you this help. Magic that strong, and knowledge of the past and of my father's secrets... It is beyond that of mortals."

I frowned. "You mean... The gods?"

He turned back to the aisle. "It does not matter. What matters is that we keep going, and find the mist-staff."

I scowled. "Of course it matters. You're suggesting

the ancient gods who vanished centuries ago might be interested in us?"

"The gods have played with mortals for all of time. If I am a mere pawn in a game, I would rather not know." He began to walk back down the aisle, and I felt a jolt of reluctance to leave the church. His tone was still clipped and cold, but the dangerous edge was gone. Perhaps now was a good time to try to talk to him.

"You wish to control your own fate?" I moved quickly to catch him up.

"I wish to find the mist-staff," he said.

"In order to control your fate." I pushed.

"Yes. Which is why I need you and your visions."

Him telling me he needed me sent a thrill through me that didn't match the sting of the fact that he had his back to me when he said it. No care or compassion. Perfunctory and practical. He needed me because I was being sent the information we needed to find the mist-staff.

"Tell me what happened with your—"

Mazrith strode out of the church before I could finish the question.

CHAPTER 5
REYNA

Voror was waiting for me on the other side of the bridge, which Mazrith let me cross alone again, his shadow snakes steadying me instead of his own arms. "If I fell off, that would teach him a lesson." I repeated my chant: one foot after the other. "Then how would he get his stupid mist-staff?"

"The magic stopped me joining you," Voror said as soon as my feet were back on the stone. I pressed my hands to the ground quickly, sending another prayer of thanks to Freya that I'd made it across.

"Yes, I think there is something about only royals being permitted," I told the owl, straightening.

"Then why were you able to cross?"

"Good question." Mazrith was already marching back to the palace tower. "Why was I allowed onto the island when I'm not royal?" I called, hurrying after him.

"You bear my mark."

I glanced down at the black rune on my wrist. A swell of unwanted emotion filled me, and I dropped my arm.

Nobody could overhear us up here. I wanted answers. I *deserved* answers.

"I think I know what happened," I said, loud enough that I knew Mazrith could hear me.

He didn't slow.

I continued on. "Your mother sacrificed herself for you."

His steps halted. His shoulders lifted and didn't drop. They just stayed high, tense. Solid. An impenetrable wall of anger and... denial? Regret?

"You needed her magic to hide what you really are, and she gave up her life to give it to you."

Slowly, he turned to face me. His expression was void of anything compassionate, and when he spoke his voice was ice. "I understand that you are not choosing to see into my past. But that does not give you a right to it."

His words stung. I had given him all my secrets. "Am I right?" I asked. He just stared. "If I am, then it is not a curse you seek to break at all. It is a way to replace what she gave you when it runs out." His chest rose and fell, but still he didn't speak. "How was she hiding it before, when you were younger? Why did it have to come to..." The image of him and the dagger flashed into my mind. "That?"

"All you need to know is that I will become what you saw when the last golden rune leaves my skin," he hissed. "The rest is irrelevant."

31

My mouth fell open. "How is it irrelevant? It is who you are!"

"It is irrelevant," he ground out.

"And you called me a hypocrite? You have been pushing and pushing to find out what I am, yet you refuse to tell me what you are?"

"What *you* are could be integral to us completing this quest. I know what I am, and I need a mist-staff to survive. To get the mist-staff, I need you. It is that simple." His blazing eyes bore into mine as hurt surged through me.

"That's all I am to you?" Shadows swirled across his eyes. He didn't answer. "This time it is you who is lying," I spat. "I know you meant every word you have said to me since I got here. You care about me more than my worth in this quest." As my words formed, my gut twisted. I hadn't realized how desperately I wanted to believe what I was saying until I had heard the plea in my own voice.

"It is all irrelevant," he repeated, his conviction less, the grate in his voice more.

"No." I folded my arms across my chest, trying to keep my voice calm. "The pool, your words, your *touch*... It was real. I know it was real."

He looked like he was going to step toward me and I firmed my feet, but he stayed where he was. "What is *real* is what you saw in that vision. I am a murderer, and a monster."

"No—" I shook my head, trying to cut in, but he

spoke over me, louder, his teeth gritted tight together and the words forced from his lips.

"Until that is righted, there is no us. No words. No touch. Do you understand me?"

I drew in air, trying to control my emotions. "Righted? What do you mean, righted?

"I must avenge her death and honor her sacrifice."

"By finding the mist-staff?"

"Yes."

"And then?"

"And then, we start again."

I threw my arms up, frustration besting me. "But nothing has changed! You are no different from who you were in the pool just a day ago. Why do you need to behave like this now, so cold and hard and—"

Emotion flared in his eyes. "Everything has changed!" He shouted the words, his own control snapping.

"No, I just know more about you now, that doesn't mean—"

Again he cut me off, this time shadows bursting from his staff. "I am a murderer and a monster, and there is no us until that is righted!" His shadows had formed a snake as he shouted, and it was wrapping itself around his shoulders, as though protecting him.

From me? From my judgement?

Tears were burning in my eyes, though I knew they wouldn't fall. "Maz, I do not believe you are a monster." I kept my voice quiet, my tone as level as I could. "Please. Nothing has changed."

The snake coiled tighter around him. "Will you help me find the mist-staff?"

"Of course I will."

"Then there is nothing else to discuss." He turned away from me, striding to the tower.

I glared at his back, willing my roiling emotions not to tip into anger.

I couldn't force him to talk to me. But that wouldn't stop me trying to convince him that I didn't believe he was a monster.

The vivid memory bubbled up of what he had done to the guard after the snake had bitten me.

And the man in Slaithewaite he sent mad.

Worse was the image of him rage-filled and holding the dagger lingering relentlessly at the forefront of my mind.

I had felt different my whole life, and the reactions of those around me had changed me; made me angry, defensive. Stronger, maybe, but full of hate and fear.

Mazrith had been through far more than having red hair in a sea of brown.

What might that have done to him?

CHAPTER 6

REYNA

M uch as I longed to, I didn't try to talk to Mazrith on the way down to the shrine. His brooding silence, along with Voror's occasional beak clicks and my restless shifting made for an awkward journey. At least the cube made it a short one.

Crossing the arm out over the chasm was no easier than last time I'd done it, especially coming straight after the awful invisible bridge. I shuffled across on my backside and was slightly heartened that Mazrith helped me up when I reached the palm housing the ring of statues. I was less heartened that he wouldn't look at me to receive my smile of thanks.

"Which statue needs fixing?" He looked around at the eight solemn stone figures.

The 'star stone' rune I had seen had floated from the middle faceless statue. I moved toward it cautiously. The staff the figure was holding was a mess of broken stone, some of it worn and some of it jagged and sharp. I could see nowhere that a star stone, or even a gem of any kind, would fit. I rubbed at the stone staff-top, trying to see if there was gold underneath, but the stone was unyielding.

Mazrith moved behind me, and a surge of longing to step back into him took me by surprise. Could I convince him to open up with physical contact?

Before I could decide if it was a good or a terrible idea, he reached over my shoulder and pressed a finger to the center of the statue's collarbone, the hollow at the bottom of its throat.

"There is an indent here."

He was right. His hand disappeared behind me, then reappeared a beat later, the star stone between his fingertips. Carefully, he held the stone to the indent.

A blinding flash of light made me throw my arms over my eyes and stumble back into his huge body. His hands gripped my shoulders and I heard him give a hiss of pain. He was more sensitive to light than I was, but he'd steadied me instead of shielding his own eyes.

The light dimmed enough for me to take my arm away, but when I looked at the statue it was just a glowing blob of light that made my eyes stream to look at.

"What are we supposed to—"

"Should the seeker of this staff be true

Those worthy of such power are few
Injustice and cruelty spurned
Magic of the soul is earned"

The ringing voice carried through the cavern, then with a clatter, the stone of the statue's staff fell away, revealing a simple wooden rod. I squinted at it, the statue's light still too bright to make out any details.

"Is that... Is that the staff?" I whispered into the silence that followed the statues words.

Mazrith didn't answer, instead slowly stepping around me, shielding his eyes, and reaching for the wooden staff.

My heart flipped in my chest as he closed his fingers around the wood and lifted it away from the statue.

Had we actually done it?

Had we found the all-powerful staff that would allow him to overthrow his stepmother, save himself, and end the *Leikmot*?

He turned his back to the bright light, lifted the staff in one hand and his shadow-staff in the other, then closed his eyes. Shadows whirled around his own staff, spinning faster and faster. He tipped his head back, and I saw his grip on both staffs tighten.

Then, the shadows stopped.

With a rush, they returned to the skull on the top of his staff, and Mazrith opened his eyes.

I couldn't help flinching.

He looked furious. Perhaps as furious as when I'd had the last vision inside the waterfall.

"What's wrong?"

"This is the staff we seek. And it will not respond to me."

I had made staffs my whole adult life, and there was only one reason I knew of that a staff would not respond to a fae. "It does not recognize you as its owner."

Mazrith only growled in answer.

"How do you claim it as your own?"

"I don't know," he said, through bared teeth.

"The riddle said the seeker of the staff must be true, and it would spurn injustice and cruelty. Perhaps you need to prove to it that you are worthy?"

Mazrith's face contorted. "I am not true! I am the embodiment of an infernal lie!" He thrust the staff at me, rage lining his every feature. "This is an impossible fucking game, designed by twisted deities who like to torture their toys!"

I took the staff from him, feeling nothing magical at all about the rod of wood. "Mazrith, calm down—"

"This infernal fucking quest was doomed from the start." Shadows burst out once more from his staff and swirled around him. I moved to lay my hand on his chest but he stepped back, out of my reach.

His eyes were narrowed against the light from the statue, and his neck and shoulders were so tight he looked like he might explode, shatter into pieces.

"Just like last time, a vision will come and show us what to do," I said, as soothingly as possible.

"You do not even know who is sending these visions, and yet you blindly trust them! You are a fool."

"Don't take your frustration out on me," I snapped back, trying to school my flash of anger. "I'm trying to help you. And you know perfectly well that the visions can be trusted; they've got us this far."

He snarled and banged his staff down on the palm. "You are not who you appear to be. I am not who I appear to be. This is a mess of lies and deceit and secrets. I have had enough."

"Maz, please, calm down. We are so close. We have the staff."

"And we cannot wield it." He dragged the words out.

I tried to ignore the fact that he was talking to me like I was stupid. He was the one person who had told me he didn't think I was stupid.

"A vision will show us what to do," I repeated.

"I cannot be around that fucking statue any longer," he said, jabbing his staff at the brightly lit statue. "We are leaving."

"You know, I'm starting to understand how annoying it was when I was trying to be difficult," I said quietly as we rode the cube back up to the palace.

Mazrith gave a hiss of breath but didn't speak.

"I'm trying to help you. I'm right here, doing this with you. Please, talk to me. When we work together, we do so well."

I paused as the cube opened and he stepped out onto the mountain ledge. It was dark, and I caught his arm, turning him so that I could see his face in the gloom. I needed him looking at me, needed him to know I meant my next words. "You know I don't care what you look like, right? This world of beautiful, glittering fae you grew up in, it's not the same as mine. I care about your actions, not your face."

Pain shone in his eyes. Not hope, or relief, or any other emotion I had hoped my words would elicit. "My actions are no better than my true face." I barely heard his words, they were so quiet.

"I do not believe that. What happened to you? Were you born like that?"

"Nobody is born like that," he spat. "And even if they were, no Court in the land would let a being like that live."

"That is not true either," I said, though with less conviction. Would the people of *Yggdrasil* let someone who looked like that prove themselves worthy? Or would the greed and vanity that had spread through *Yggdrasil* like a plague mean he would never have stood a chance?

Mazrith's face twisted bitterly. "My Court will not accept me when my mother's magic runs out. The Queen will rule. You will die." Darkness filled his eyes, danger

40

oozing from every pore of his body. Every instinct told me to run. To hide.

I tightened my grip on his arm.

"We will find a way to use the mist-staff, and that will not come to pass."

He pulled his arm from my grip.

"Mazrith—"

But once again, he turned away from me.

CHAPTER 7

REYNA

Mazrith refused to say anything else to me all the way back to the Serpent Suites. When we entered, he strode straight through to the war room, picked up a bag, and then left.

I snatched a cushion from the chair and launched it at the door he had just slammed.

"Glad to see you're taking out your frustration on something that deserves it," Frima said as she came into the room, eyeing the cushion, then the wooden staff still clutched to my side.

"Unlike that *heimskr*," I snarled, jutting my chin out at the door. "Fates, and I thought *I* could be obstinate."

She laughed. "Want to train?"

"Yes," I said, instantly.

It was probably not what I needed to do — I had to talk with my friends and Voror, and find a way to make

COURT OF SERPENTS AND SECRETS

Maz and the stupid unresponsive mist-staff see eye-to-eye. But what I wanted to do was train.

We practiced with the bow until I could barely lift my arms, and I poured every ounce of anger, frustration and determination into each move I made, relishing in the control and power I had when the weapon was in my hands. I had learned to fight in the taverns, watching humans wrestle and argue over ale or games or lovers, but I had always been limited by my size and strength. The only real weapon I had considered that set me apart was my ability to rile and annoy folk into making mistakes or losing their temper.

But the bow... It made me feel even more powerful than the staff had. The *thunk* it made when the arrow hit the target was so final, so satisfyingly dangerous. The arrow's power was not limited by the strength of my arms or the speed of my swipe, but by my aim and the control in my body.

"You hit nine of the ten moving targets on the last round," Frima said as she cleared the mess of straw from the training room floor. "Next time we will go out on horseback and practice in the forest."

"Why didn't we do that today?" The thought of riding Rasa filled me with restless excitement.

"Next time. Maz will take you riding before we go to the Earth Court, I'm sure."

"I wouldn't bet on it. When do we leave?"

43

"No communication has been announced yet," she shrugged.

Brynja had a bath drawn for me when we returned, and soaking in the hot water felt good. I asked her if I could eat alone in my room and when a cheese pie the size of my head and a carafe of nettle wine had been delivered, I looked up at the rafters. "Voror?"

He fluttered down and settled on the bed post.

"Can you eat and speak at the same time?" he asked, distaste in his tone as I shoveled amazing pastry covered in gooey melted cheese into my mouth.

"Yes," I answered around a mouthful of food.

"I shall rephrase. *Should* you eat and speak at the same time?"

"Sorry Voror. If you want to know what's been going on, you'll have to share my attention with this joyous pie."

I told him everything that had happened on the other side on the waterfall in the tree, and filled in the few gaps he had since then, including the conversation inside the church. I held back nothing, and although I felt a stab of guilt at sharing Mazrith's secrets, I consoled myself with the fact that I had to talk to someone, and Mazrith had removed himself as an option. If he wasn't so busy refusing to talk to me, I wouldn't be spilling everything to a magical owl.

"So, the prince is not a shadow-fae or a gold-fae?" Voror said thoughtfully.

"That's what he said."

"And he was not born that way. That implies someone or something changed him. Interesting. And he appears to have lost hope at the mist-staff rejecting him. Without hope, fear thrives."

I swallowed down some wine, trying to cling to my optimism.

"Do you think it really rejected him? Or just hasn't recognized him as its owner yet?"

"I know little of such things." His head turned slowly to where the staff was propped up against my dressing table. "I would not let it leave your sight, even for a moment. And you might talk to the annoying *shadow-spinner*."

I nodded. "Yes. All good ideas."

"I have many of those."

I didn't argue with him. He did have good ideas, to be fair. "Do you think Mazrith is right, and the gods are sending me the visions?" If he was, then maybe I was human after all.

"It was not a god who visited me."

"You're sure?"

He paused before answering. "I suppose a god can take whatever form they wish."

I sighed. "Whoever it is, let us hope they send me something useful soon. Like how to make a mist-staff become more than a wooden stick."

But, no vision came. Three days passed, and after the first, I began to worry. I spent time with Kara in the library, trawling through every book I could find that might have mention of mist-staffs, or staff craft. I found nothing helpful.

Ellisar accompanied us on every trip, and I got the impression that he had enjoyed being Kara's chaperone when I had been away in the Ice Court. I saw him stealing long glances at her that might explain her flush and giggles when he found a reason to talk to her. I wanted to ask her about the huge warrior, but either Lhoris or Ellisar himself always seemed to be around.

Mazrith appeared for dinner with everyone in the war room the first night, but he spoke to nobody. When Frima gave him the same good-natured banter she had always given him over the dinner table, he picked up his plate and left the room, shoulders tense and high. I knocked on the door of the room he was staying in since he gave up his own room for me, but he did not answer.

The next day, Frima and I trained again, this time with staffs and swords. I asked her to take me out on horseback with the bow, but she was reluctant, and I was sure it was because she knew Maz had taken me riding before.

"Maz won't mind," I told her. "He's not going to take me himself. He's being a pigheaded, stubborn *heimskr*."

But she insisted we practiced with the staff instead.

I had followed Voror's advice, taking the wooden mist-staff with me everywhere, relieved that the only bit of magic it did seem to have was the ability to compact down like the other staffs of *Yggdrasil* did. I spent time studying it, but there was nothing but wood to look at. No gems, no carvings, no indents. Just a piece of wood that shrank when I held it to my belt.

When Mazrith didn't show up for dinner on the second evening, I banged on his door repeatedly until he finally opened it.

"What do you want?" His hair was not as tidy as usual, and dark bags under his eyes marred his beautiful face. He had no furs on, just black trousers and an open black shirt. His many amulets hung around his neck, Thor's Talisman amongst them. I forced my eyes from his chest to his face.

"You to try and bond with the mist-staff," I said bluntly. "As far as I'm aware, there's not one in your room, so why are you locking yourself in there?" Shadows swirled across his tight eyes.

"Leave. I do not wish to talk to you."

"You *have* to talk to me. I'm the only one who can help you, and right now I'm the only one of us trying."

"You do not know that."

"You're right, because you won't fucking talk to me." His face mirrored my frustration. "What have you been doing since we got back?"

"It does not concern you."

My mouth fell open and I only just stopped myself punching him. "Everything you do concerns me, Mazrith. What the fates is wrong with you?"

"You know exactly what is wrong with me. And so does the staff. Now, leave me alone."

CHAPTER 8

REYNA

The following day I went to visit Tait. I would have loved to have gone to the village on Rasa, but Frima had insisted we go by carriage, waiting outside when we reached the alley that housed his workshop.

I found the chaos of Tait's building strangely calming. The clutter should have felt overwhelming, or claustrophobic, things hanging from the ceiling and filling the floor and benches, but instead I felt like I could never be bored in the space.

"You have come to find out what was in the Ice Court sphere?" Tait said as I closed the door behind me.

"No." I shook my head. "But if you have anything to share I'll gladly listen?"

"I am afraid not. I have no idea how to get into the infernal thing." A scowl replaced his usual grin.

"You'll work it out, Tait, I'm sure."

"Hmm. So, to what do I owe the pleasure of your visit? Have you come to observe me spinning?" His face lit up. "Or have you come to show me how you work with gold?"

"Again, no, sorry Tait. I've come to ask you about mist-staffs."

His face lit up. "You are close to finding one?"

Caution made me pause. If Mazrith had not already spoken to him, I should tread carefully. "Tait, I'm sure you'll understand that I have to be vague with you."

His nose twitched, but he nodded. "I understand."

"We have found a riddle regarding the staff."

"Riddle?"

"Should the seeker of the staff be true

Those worthy of such power are few

Injustice and cruelty spurned

Magic of the soul is earned."

Tait pushed his glasses up his nose, then stuck his little finger in his mouth, screwing up his face in thought. "I assume it is the same for gold-fae staffs, but the process of ownership of a shadow-fae staff comes down to wealth."

I nodded. "Yes. If you provide the material, the staff is yours. I have only seen one rejected, and that was when the staff had been used to kill a female, then passed on to her widower. We melted down the gold and reused it, but the staff must have retained the memory."

"Yes, yes, I have had similar experiences when repurposing materials. But a mist-staff... They were created by the gods themselves, using material from the mists of creation."

I had read as much in the library, though references to them had been incredibly scant and mostly referred to them as myth. "They gave one to each of the fae courts."

Tait turned and began to rummage through a pile of belongings on a table. Eventually he held his hand aloft triumphantly. A green leather-bound book was clutched in his fingers.

"I got this ten years ago from an exiled Earth Court noble." His eyes glinted. "He had stolen many things from the palace before he fled."

I stepped close, reaching for it. Tait's hands tightened on it a moment, then he relinquished his grip. "It contains everything I know about mist-staffs, amongst other stories about the gods departure from *Yggdrasil*." Curiosity surged through me.

"Thank you. I'll return it as soon as I'm done."

"Be sure that you do. In the meantime, I can tell you that there were ten mist-staffs made. As you said, one was given to each of the Courts initially, along with to the other races of *Yggdrasil*."

I held a hand up, signaling him to pause. "The other races?"

"Yes. Dwarves, wolves, and the high fae, or Vanir as the gods called them. That made eight. Then the goddess Freya and the mighty Thor took one each for themselves."

"And now we only know the whereabouts of one," I said. *Two, if you counted the one on my hip.*

"Indeed, though I suspect they are camouflaged throughout *Yggdrasil*."

I had seen the Gold Court Queen's staff and knew for certain that wasn't a mist-staff. Could the royal families of the earth, ice and fire courts have held on to theirs? Or was one of theirs tucked into my belt? I wondered how many powerful figures from *Yggdrasil's* history might have wielded it.

"Do you think a mist-staff is able to choose or reject its owner?"

"That riddle suggests so." Tait peered into my eyes intently. "You have found it, haven't you? Why else would you have been given those words?"

I stepped back. "I have been given a lot that I am not sure what to do with."

"Your visions?"

I nodded. "Somebody is helping me."

Tait cocked his head, and said nothing, chewing on the end of his finger again. "If the staff has rejected Mazrith, I am afraid there may be severe consequences."

My gut tightened. "You don't think Mazrith is worthy? You think he is cruel or unjust?"

The *shadow-spinner* shook his head sadly. "No, Reyna. I would not have given you that book if it were not that it may help my oldest friend. The Prince is not cruel. But, he is not true. There is darkness in him."

There was darkness in me too. Tait knew nothing of

my connection to the Starved Ones, or the Elder's desire for me. For a beat, I considered telling him. But, seemingly of their own volition, my lips stayed tightly shut.

Tait sighed. "I pray the fates will guide you to your answer, Reyna, for both your sakes."

"What happened to him?" The question escaped before I could stop it.

"That is not my tale to tell. And besides, I do not know. Only suspect."

I suppressed a grunt of frustration, and switched subjects. "Mazrith thinks my visions may be sent by the gods, because they contain knowledge of things that could not be seen by a mortal."

"Like the King hiding his valuables inside *Yggdrasil*?"

"Exactly."

"It is possible," Tait mused. "But, your quest goes beyond removing the Queen from power and saving the Prince's life, if that is true."

My stomach squirmed. Voror's mysterious fae's words, and whatever the fates I had to do with the Starved Ones powered to the front of my thoughts.

Was Mazrith supposed to get the staff to help me? Perhaps with the mist-staff, Mazrith could find out why the hideous creatures wanted me. Perhaps, to save *Yggdrasil* we were supposed to vanquish them once and for all?

Hope surged in me at the idea, though it was accompanied by an uneasy gut-deep sense of foreboding. It was me who was connected to them, not Mazrith. A sickening certainty that my fate was tied with theirs rose in me, and for a moment my vision darkened. I gripped the nearest table, but light filtered back through, the room becoming clear again.

"Are you alright?" Tait's voice was filled with concern.

Had I been about to have a vision of the Starved Ones, triggered by thinking about them? *Or, had I been about to have a vision that might actually have helped us?*

Feeling a mixture of relief and regret that the vision hadn't taken hold, I blinked at Tait.

"Yes, I'm fine. Sorry." I held the book up. "I had better get to reading. Thank you for your help, Tait."

"If it will help the Prince, then you are more than welcome."

"Oh, one more thing, before I leave," I said, suddenly remembering. "The mark on your wrist." I pointed, and he raised his arm and blinked at the rune.

"Yes?"

"Does it have any other use or significance in the Shadow Court?"

He shook his head. "No. This mark is for the rune-marked alone. It is the same in your court, is it not?"

"Yes," I said slowly. "I suppose." There were more than a dozen runes that meant gold, it was so important to the gold-fae, but the one on my wrist only appeared on the rune-marked. "Have there ever been any shadow-spinners in the royal family?"

Tait looked at me like I'd lost my mind. "Royal

shadow-spinners? Rune-marked are human, Reyna, and the Shadow Court has never had a human as part of the royal family. Until now," he added, cocking his head at me.

"We're not married yet," I murmured.

Why would that rune have appeared on the tapestry? I was sure it meant something. Shrugging, I thanked Tait again.

"Take care, Reyna," he said.

But as I took a step toward the door to his workshop, blackness dropped over my vision.

When it cleared, I was in the berserker's cavern under the mountain. I wasn't looking at it as a memory, I realized. I was looking at it through somebody's eyes. *Mazrith's eyes.*

Was he there now?

"Why?" The Prince's voice boomed through the cavern, and a torrent of emotion flooded through me as he hurled shadow magic at the colossal axe of the statue.

Regret, grief, fear.

But mostly rage.

The statue stood huge and silent, as Mazrith hammered it with power.

"Why her?" he bellowed, his voice fading as the vision lifted.

I sucked in air, hands clutched into fists and my heart pounding.

Such rage. Enough that I felt it seeping through me, making my whole body tense and tight.

"Reyna, what did you see?" Tait was clinging to my shirt-sleeve, peering at me.

"Mazrith."

"What kind of vision was it? Is he alright?"

"No, I don't think he is." Knowing he was trapped in that kind of emotional turmoil was too much. I was done giving him space.

The Prince of the Shadow Court would tell me his secrets, or Freya help me, I'd kill him myself.

CHAPTER 9
REYNA

I t took little time to get back to the palace, but my determination to have it out with Mazrith grew ever stronger on the journey. Whatever it took, I would get through to the shadow prince that I was his ally. That together we would find a way to use the mist-staff.

It was only once we were back to the Serpent Suites it occurred to me that I could not get down to the berserker's cavern without shadow magic. I briefly considered asking Frima, but Mazrith had told me that the caverns inside the mountain were his secret, and I didn't want to betray his trust.

Reluctantly, I decided to wait for him in his rooms. I could read Tait's book until he returned and might even have something good to tell him.

Frima came to a dead stop in the middle of the corridor. I halted too, on edge. "What—"

I never finished my question.

Shadows wrapped around my entire body, and then I couldn't see a thing. Wails and screams filled my ears, and then images began forming on the back of my eyelids, which were clamped shut against the stinging shadows.

They were images of Lhoris and Kara, strung up in the Queen's throne room, spread out on the racks hanging from the cavernous ceiling. Blood dripped down from both of their bodies, and it was *my* skin, *my* face, *my* lips, it reached. The version of me in the image raised a hand, and Kara convulsed, screaming.

Bile rose in my throat, horror and revulsion taking over my body at what I was seeing.

It was more than seeing it, I was *living* it, a waking dream.

The me in the image flicked my hand, and bones cracked.

My head swam, horror making sure I'd be sick.

I couldn't live this in my mind, I couldn't.

I tried to scream, but I didn't know if any sound came out.

The images blurred as I desperately tried to force them out, tried to stop them, tried to remove them from my brain.

But still they came. Me, torturing the only two people I had ever loved. Relishing it.

"Stop! Please, stop!" I roared the words, and this time, I heard them tearing from my chest.

Some conscious part of me stirred, and I grasped for reality.

Shadow magic was making me see this.

Pain lanced through my head, spearing me like an arrow. I was vaguely aware of my knees hitting the carpet, and then more screams.

For a second, I thought the screams were Kara's in the image, or mine. But with a flash of light, the images vanished, and the pain in my skull with it.

The scream continued.

I opened my eyes.

A hooded figure was mirroring my position, kneeling on the floor.

Mazrith stood over him, shadows flowing from his staff and circling the man, swirling into his eyes, ears, throat.

My vision clouded again, and I thought the hooded fae had sent more images. But instead, I was seeing what the figure was seeing.

Children. *His own children?*

They were drowning in blood.

"Stop!" he shrieked, his fear and horror overwhelming me before the vision fled my mind.

Realization smacked into me as I blinked through stinging tears.

Mazrith was doing what the fae had just done to me. He was torturing him, making him see his worst fears.

"Mazrith, stop!" I sprang to my feet, but Mazrith didn't turn to me. The hooded fae kept screaming, and I saw a door open along the corridor, and Svangrior running out. Frima stood to one side, staff raised and eyes filled with uncertainty. "Stop!" I yelled again.

"He was sent to torture and kill you." Mazrith's voice actually sounded like a snake's hiss. "He doesn't deserve to breathe the same air as you."

"So lock him up and find out who sent him! You don't need to torture him!"

His eyes snapped to mine, and I sucked in a breath. They were filled with black. Not shadows, but solid, soulless black. He flicked his staff, and there was a snapping sound. The man's neck slumped at an impossible angle, his scream ending abruptly before his body crumpled to the floor.

Revulsion surged up through my stomach as the vivid image of Orm so casually ending the warrior woman's life on the carpet in the Gold Court palace flooded back to me.

"You're not one of them," I choked, not needing him to believe the words, but myself.

"Deal with this," Mazrith barked to Svangrior, as he skidded to a stop. He looked between us, and then at the body. The fae's hood had fallen back when his neck had snapped. He was a shadow-fae, young and handsome.

Mazrith stamped toward his rooms, his shadows following.

"What happ—"

I didn't stay to answer Svangrior, propelling myself after Mazrith instead.

"Everybody, out!" he bellowed as soon as he entered the Suites. Nobody hesitated to obey, and I was so fixed on him I didn't take a second to send a reassuring glance at my friends or Brynja as they raced from the room.

"You are not one of them," I said again, loudly, as the door slammed closed. "Please, Mazrith, tell me you are not one of them. Because the only time I have ever seen such reckless care for life was by Lord Orm."

He whirled, rage on his face. "Oh Reyna, of course I am one of them! In fact, I'm worse. I'm everything you've heard I am and more."

"Lies!"

He spread his arms. "That man was going to kill you. He would have tortured you, and killed you, on the orders of another. That is what the fae do. They are worthless, greedy, honorless vermin. And I am a Prince of the fae. More than that, I am a *true* monster, a product of lies and hatred and greed."

I stared at him, tears filling my eyes. "No. No, you're the first fae I've met who is none of those things."

"I am all of those things. You've even had the privilege of seeing me kill my own mother." Rage and bitterness deformed his beautiful face, and pale scars began to stand out on his skin.

"Mazrith, stop. Stop all of this. You are angry because you didn't want me to see that. I understand. But that doesn't mean—"

"Listen to me," he growled, power rolling from his words. "It is a matter of weeks until this world sees what

61

I truly am. And I will not hide. I will not let them burn me, or kill you. If they will not accept me, then they shall learn to fear me."

Everything about him had changed.

The cold, rigid control of the last few days had been unnerving, but this? This was unbridled rage, dangerous power teetering on the edge of madness.

"You would become like your stepmother?"

"I will become whatever I was meant to be."

"You were meant to be *good*. Honorable. Worthy of the god's respect, and the loyalty and love of your Court, not their fear. This isn't you."

He stepped toward me, and I couldn't help but step back. No courage in the world could stand up to the furious power he was emitting. "You do not know me, little human."

I felt sick as I stared up into his manic gaze. "I will not stand by you if this is the path you choose."

"You have no choice." He raised his wrist, displaying the black mark etched in his skin. The matching one on my own skin burned white hot.

The tears spilled from my eyes, my gut wrenching.

He was right.

I didn't know him. Everything I had come to believe in was being torn to shreds with each word he spoke.

"Leave." My word was choked.

He glowered down at me, black eyes fixed on my face. When he didn't move, I turned, running for the door to the bedroom. Painfully aware that it was *his* bedroom, and I had nowhere of my own to go, I yanked open the door, and slammed it closed behind me.

The sound of breaking glass and splintering wood made me jump, and then silence descended.

CHAPTER 10

REYNA

When the sobs started, I was devastated to discover that they wouldn't stop. An hour must have passed before I heard a knock on the door.

I didn't respond, but it creaked open anyway. Hoping to see Kara, my stomach sank when Frima poked her head around the door.

She raised her eyebrows at me, then shouldered open the door the rest of the way to reveal two large glasses of something in each hand.

I sucked down air, trying to stop my tears as she sat on the bed next to me and passed me a glass.

"Whisky," she said. "You know the fae he killed was an assassin?"

I took a tentative sip of the drink, not really enjoying the burn that stole its way down my chest. "Yeah.

Mazrith said he was sent to kill me. Before he... you know. Snapped his neck in half."

"Death happens here, Reyna. Especially to known, wanted court assassins."

I frowned at her. "I'm not crying because someone who tried to kill me died."

"Oh. Good."

I took another sip. "I'm crying because I thought Mazrith was something he isn't. Or because he's becoming something he shouldn't. I'm not sure which." Frima said nothing, and I found myself continuing. "He knows I value my freedom above everything. And he waved this infernal fucking mark at me like a bully and a... a captor. No better than that bastard who tried to bind me before him."

"I think that bastard wanted to bind you for different reasons than Maz did," she said gently.

That was true. Mazrith's motivations had been to keep me safe, I was fairly sure. But that didn't change the fact that he had just embodied everything I hated about Orm, and about his stepmother.

"He threatened to rule the Shadow Court through fear."

This time Frima frowned. "Then I can answer your first question. He is becoming something else. Because the Maz I know wouldn't do or say that."

I felt a flicker of relief that I hadn't been tricked in the short time I had been here, that I had read him and his relationship with his warriors correctly. "How long have you known him?"

"Nearly a hundred years."

I let out a sigh. It was so easy to forget how long-lived the fae were. "And has he always been honest and honorable?"

"Perhaps a little rage-filled and violent at times, but yes, he was always honorable. He is like his mother was. It was incredibly hard for him when she died."

I looked at her, eyes stinging. "How did she die?"

"A disease. One of the rare few that can kill fae. He always believed his stepmother caused it somehow."

"Caused a disease?"

Frima let out a long breath. "Please, don't tell Mazrith. But Svangrior, Ellisar, and I all know more than he thinks we do. We know his stepmother's staff is unbeatable. And we know she probably contrived to kill his mother, and then his father. It is possible that she is strong enough to have triggered a disease."

"What else do you know?"

"That something has been wrong since she died. His temper, his humor, his obsession with finding you becoming so urgent."

I paused at her words. "He began searching for me when his mother died, right?"

"No."

"What?" He had told me his mother had shown him the shrine and the inscription before she died, and that was when he started looking for the *copper-haired gold-giver*.

"He was searching for a red-headed human for a long time. The last ten years maybe. Five years ago, when his mother died, he told us he had discovered you were a *gold-giver*, which narrowed it down somewhat."

So, there were still more secrets he had kept from me. "Frima, he looked crazy today. His eyes went black, like the Queen's."

"I saw."

"What sent his stepmother mad?"

"Nobody knows. She was unhinged when she wormed her way into court. It was not surprising his father fell for her—he wasn't exactly a shining example of sanity."

"Mazrith told me he disliked his father."

"Dislike does not come close. His father was cruel, power hungry — nothing like his mother. I... I probably should not share this but Mazrith was on the receiving end of his father's cruelty often."

My stomach twisted as I remembered the vision of the young Mazrith, hiding behind the berserker axe under the mountain.

All those scars... Had his father caused those? I felt sick again.

"How the fates did he end up normal at all?" I had mumbled the words aloud, and Frima answered.

"His mother. Friends like me and Svangrior and

Ellisar. Tait. He's clever, too. He reads, he learns. He took solace in the ancient teachings of honor and valor."

Without meaning to, I gripped her hand. "Frima, please. We can't let him become like his stepmother or Orm. He believes he is...something he is not." Would she still follow him, love him as her leader, if she saw what was under his mother's magic? "We have to keep him sane, even if.... Even if he changes."

Her eyes filled with the compassion I had longed to see in Mazrith's.

"You love him," she said softly.

I shook my head. "No. I can't."

"You sound like a person in love."

"I am bound to him. Unwillingly. That can never be love. But I can't let him become a monster. He deserves so much more. As do you, your friends, this Court. *Yggdrasil.*"

She pulled me into a hug, making me spill my drink. "I will stand by him, Reyna. And, by you. You have my loyalty."

Mercifully, she couldn't see the fresh tears that sprang to my eyes at her words.

"I am grateful that my body does not produce the things your human ones do." Voror's voice floated into my head, then he swooped down onto the bed post.

Frima ended our hug to gave him a wary look, then fixed her attention back on me. "I have to go. You'll be okay talking to your... owl? I can send in Kara."

"No, thank you. I need to talk with Voror."

She nodded and rose. "Whatever it is you and Maz are doing, I have faith in you both. Remember that."

She squeezed my braid and smiled at me, then left.

"Do you have faith in you both?" asked the owl.

"I don't know what to think any more. Do you think he could do what he threatened? Become... like the rest of them?"

"Yes. I believe he could."

"Do you think he will?" I rephrased the question. I had no doubt that he *could*, either.

"I do not know."

"Voror, do you think Mazrith's mother was already dying? Of that disease Frima just mentioned? That way, Mazrith ending her life.... It is not the same, if she was already dying."

Voror's beak clicked slowly. "Yes. I think that is very likely. A mercy killing that ensured her power could be passed to him."

My heart ached for him, and it was so much stronger than the anger he had made me feel.

"He is no murderer. I'm sure of it." The assassin's body flashed into my head.

"That creature deserved death," Voror said, his feathers ruffling. "I heard the two warriors talking as they removed the body. He was well known for committing heinous acts across the Court."

"He didn't deserve to be tortured," I muttered.

"On the contrary. It sounds like he got exactly what he deserved."

"Freya help me," I sighed, slumping back onto the mattress and rubbing my hands across my stinging eyes. "How can I stop him? Is this how I was meant to save *Yggdrasil*? Stop Mazrith becoming a tyrant?"

"I do not believe that to be your only purpose, but that task may well have fallen to you."

"How can I get through to him? He is so impenetrable." I banged my fists on the blankets uselessly. "He needs forgiveness. Absolution. And I can't give him that. Well, I can, but it doesn't mean enough to him."

Voror hooted softly, and I sat up. He hardly ever hooted. "*Ravensstar*," he said, his voice faraway.

"What? The island?"

"Yes." Voror blinked at me. "We are not alone in this, Reyna." Excitement laced his words now, and before I could ask what he meant, he took off.

"Voror!" But he was gone.

CHAPTER 11

MAZRITH

"Mazrith!"

Frima's voice rang through the training room. Trust that infernal female to find me. I knew I should have gone under the mountain, where none could follow.

I launched my shadows at the dummy.

"I am busy."

She looked at the shreds of the stuffed target. "So I see. I just need a minute."

"I do not have a minute." I had a few weeks. And then, everything would change.

"She loves you."

I turned. "What?"

"She says she doesn't, but by all accounts, you just treated her like shit, and do you know what she did? She begged me to stand by you if you changed. Begged me to help stop you from going mad, like your stepmother."

71

I stared, my emotions tearing at my control as harshly as my shadows had destroyed the training dummy. "She... begged?"

"Yes. The woman who hasn't said please once since she got here responded to you being a total idiot by begging me to pledge my loyalty to you." Frima's voice softened. "Maz, she said you were...not yourself."

There was no direct question, but it was there all the same. "You do not know who I am. Nor does she."

She scowled. "I've known you since we were children."

"You know what you were supposed to know. Saw what you were supposed to see." I turned back to the dummy.

"Horseshit."

I barely kept control of the flash of rage. "Leave."

"Maz, what is going on?"

"I said, leave."

I cursed the tiny part of me, deep down, that wished she would disobey me. That she would stay. She was my closest, oldest friend. But even she didn't know what was under my mother's magic.

Reyna only knew because she had stolen the information. Taken it, without my consent.

The door closed behind me.

I roared, sending my shadows back at the dummy.

The swirling black power wouldn't obey me much longer. My mother never taught me to use my true magic; she wasn't able to.

Perhaps it would be stronger.

I snorted bitterly. Unlikely. And nothing I could wield would be strong enough to defeat my stepmother. All that talk of ruling a Court that would not accept me? It was irrelevant. The Queen was too strong. Our fates would be worse than death if she lived.

I would take Reyna, and we would run. Hide.

She wouldn't want me, but we were bound. I would be her guardhound, just as Orm had called me. Her guard*monster*. Hiding in the shadows. Keeping her safe, whether she wanted me or not.

"She begged me to stand by you if you changed." Frima's words replayed in my mind.

Was there a chance she *could* love me?

The rage inside me built. Of course she could not love me. Who could possibly be with a creature like me? I'd known it all along. If she were to have accepted me without ever seeing what I really was, then I would have deceived her. And an eternity of truth in every other part of my existence would not have made up for the fact that she would be married to a lie.

Maybe it was better this way.

Rage twisted my insides.

A single white feather floated to the floor in front of me. I picked it up, glancing at the beams of the caverned ceiling and seeing nothing.

"Your *Ravensstar* island calls you."

The voice that spoke into my mind was haughty and arrogant. "Voror?"

"Yes. There is ancient magic there. The magic of the gods."

"No magic can help me."

"It is the magic of the *Disir*."

I froze, my heart skipping. The *Disir* were the goddesses of ghosts. Of those women who fell outside of battle. Mother had always said they visited *Ravensstar's* church, but I thought she had been fanciful.

Slowly, my shadows returned to my staff.

Perhaps it would not hurt to visit the island. It was a calming place, and my mind was in turmoil.

"Prince Mazrith Andask, Lord of Snakes?"

I paused and glanced at the ceiling. "Yes?"

"The fierce lady warrior is right. Reyna does love you. She doesn't know it, or understand it. But you are responsible for more than your own fate now. Remember that."

The church was blissfully quiet. For the first time since that accursed waterfall, I felt some of the tension slipping from my muscles.

I took my time moving down the aisle, unable to stop myself glaring at the family tree tapestry.

Lies.

So many lies.

Who might I have been, if not born into the royal family of the Shadow Court?

A warrior? A scholar? A cook?

None of it mattered. I was fated to become a guard-monster.

I knelt at the altar, pressing my hands to my thighs and dipping my head.

The myths said that the *Disir* could communicate with the souls of those who had passed. Not those who had gone to the cold, dark world of *Hel*, or those who had died valiantly enough to grace the halls of *Valhalla*, but those who walked Freya's fields of the afterlife. The women who did their duty outside of the battlefield and died with a different kind of honor.

"Mother. If you can hear me... I have failed you. I found her. And you were right, she was the key. But the quest is too great, and the time too little. I... I am not worthy."

Whispering chimes rang around me, and I snapped my head up. Light had formed before me, hundreds of tiny stars making a shape that could be described as humanoid.

"The *Disir* welcome you here, Prince Mazrith," a voice sang on a breeze that blew from nowhere.

The starry figure before me shifted, and then a voice I never thought I would hear again made my heart falter. "You could never fail me, Mazrith."

"Mother? How... How is this possible?"

"You and the girl have the interest of those who can grant me this audience. I do not have long."

My mind tumbled with questions. But one word left my lips.

"Sorry." My sweating hands gripped my thighs hard enough to leave marks as I stared into the light of the otherworldly figure. I could see no features, make out no form. But I could *feel* her. My mother's spirit. "Mother, I'm so, so sorry."

"My son, it is I who owe you an apology. All those years, everything that happened to you - they were of my making, and my inability to stop him. And to force you to do what you did at the end is an abomination. That I was not cast into *Hel* is the only proof I have that my reasoning was just."

"It was all for nothing. I cannot complete the quest. And Reyna... She has seen what I truly am."

"What you truly are is what you have become, not what you hide. You have lived a life that is true, and just, and honorable. Your skin, your eyes, your face, none of that makes you a monster. Your actions make you who you are."

"That... That is what she said."

"You love her?"

"I have loved her for years."

"Then you need to let her love you in return. To refuse her love when you long for it would be a cruelty no woman deserves."

"Mother, she yearns for freedom above all else. Because of me — because I will not be able to remove the Queen from the throne — the most I can offer her is a life she will despise, hiding and running. I can't do that to her."

My mother's tone was firm when she replied. "If you were given a choice, would you wish to remain a shadow-fae?"

"Yes. I love my Court." Emotion welled in me, and blessedly, it was not rage. Laced with regret, perhaps, but not anger. "We visited the Ice Court, mother. You would have loved it."

Her reply was soft. "I am sure I would have. You intend to unite the Courts, if you regain power?"

"Of course I do. We talked for so long about the way our world might be. I have not forgotten that."

"My son, you do not understand the power you might wield. United fae... It would mean so much to *Yggdrasil*. Perhaps even enough that one day, the gods may return. You have the potential to heal so much, my son."

"I wish I could heal myself. But the staff rejected me." The anger slid back through my chest.

"Mazrith, listen to me. The healing you require will not come from magic. It will come from her. It will come from love. You must let go of this rage consuming you, and this notion that you are not worthy."

"But the staff rejecting me *proves* I am not worthy."

"I am not speaking of the staff. I am speaking of Reyna. You are worthy of her love."

"She deserves more. Better. I am a product of lies and hate and fury."

"Enough," she snapped, and the light flashed bright enough that I was forced to close my eyes. "I did not raise you to be so pigheaded or blind to the truth. Open your eyes and see what is before you. You said she values her freedom above all else?"

I blinked. "Yes."

"Then give it to her."

"I bound her to me, under threat. I can't undo a fae binding. Not without one of us dying."

"And whose magic did you use to perform that binding?"

I frowned. "Yours. All of my magic is yours."

"Last I checked, Mazrith, I do not live."

"W-what?" I straightened, confusion and some sort of hope welling inside me. "How do I—"

"I can help you no more. It is time for me to leave." The light had faded to barely a flicker, and I wasted no time arguing.

"I love you, mother. I miss you."

"I love you too, my son. Be strong. Be good. And be who she believes you to be."

CHAPTER 12

REYNA

"Reyna? Wake up."

I jerked awake, scrabbling in panic at the low voice coming from right beside me. It had taken me hours to fall asleep, my mind filled with Mazrith's black eyes and the horrific images forced into my head by the assassin.

"It's okay, Reyna, it's me. I need you to get dressed and come with me."

It was Mazrith's voice.

Relief flooded my whole system. He sounded calm, not tight and rage-filled. I blinked in the darkness, making out his figure beside my bed, his features slowly sharpening as my eyes adjusted. His irises were clear, not black.

"What do you want?" I tried to make myself sound stern, and not desperately relieved that he had come to me.

79

"To take you out riding."

My jaw fell open. "What?"

"Get dressed. I'll see you in a minute." He turned and left the room, and I could see the tension had left his shoulders.

"What in the name of Freya..."

I wasted no time dressing in my work clothes and pulling on my boots.

Something had happened, clearly. Why it meant we were going for a ride in the middle of night, I didn't know, but if he was willing to talk to me without flying into a rage, there was no way I was going to argue.

When I emerged from my room into the sitting room, he was standing by the door, dressed in black trousers and a loose black shirt. He was wearing no cloak or furs, his many amulets shining on his hard chest. The residual glow from the fireplace made it brighter than my bedroom had been, and I peered into his face for confirmation. The shadows were definitely gone. There was still tension tightening his expression, but it was more apprehensive than angry.

"What's happened?"

"Your owl," he muttered. "He is perhaps as wise as he thinks he is. And well connected."

I frowned. "What are you talking about?"

"Voror led me to an enlightening conversation. I know what I need to do now."

Hope thrilled through me, blotting out the confusion.

"To make the staff respond to you? I have it here." I patted the belt wrapped around my trousers.

He held my look a long time, then nodded toward the door. "Not here. The horses are waiting."

The horses were indeed saddled and ready when we reached the stables, Jarl holding saddlebags loaded with furs and bags. Mazrith helped me onto Rasa without a word, and she shook her mane and stamped her feet as he mounted Jarl.

"Where are we going?"

Mazrith gave the stable hands a sweeping look, then fixed his eyes on me. "Follow me. Do not go ahead."

I almost made a quip about racing him but bit my tongue. I wasn't going to push him.

I nodded instead. "Okay."

We powered through the haunted forest surrounding the palace, and I expected Mazrith to slow down when we reached Slaithewaite, suspecting that we might be visiting Tait. But, he carried on through the village, the horses hooves pounding through the sleeping hamlet. He kept driving Jarl on through the forest beyond, finally coming to a halt in a clearing that looked familiar.

"This is where we learned to jump," I breathed, once I had coaxed Rasa into stopping. Exhilaration was washing through me, as it always did when I was on the horse's powerful back.

"Yes." Mazrith vaulted from his horse, tying him to a nearby tree with the reins. I followed suit, dismounting a touch more gingerly than his graceful leap.

"Why are we here?"

"I wanted to be far from the palace. Far from anyone or anything that might overhear or interrupt us. The assassin's mind was guarded with magic. Only a powerful shadow-fae can do that. Somebody within the palace."

I swallowed. "We already knew that somebody close to us was involved. The shrine, the snake..."

"That is not what I wish to speak of. The point is, nobody is near us now. Reyna, I want to give you something."

My brows creased. "What?"

"Listen to me. Do not interrupt, and do not argue. The mist-staff will not accept me."

"Maz—"

"I told you to listen." He stepped closer to me and I stared up at him. The constant starlit skies of the Shadow Court cast dappled twilight through the canopy of trees above us, and his intense gaze caught me completely.

"I'm listening," I whispered.

"I lied to you. Rather, I omitted the truth. I have been searching for you for much longer than I let you believe. I just didn't know where to look. You have been part of my life for years, though I realize now that you never knew that you were."

I stared at him. "I met you the day you burst into my workshop. How can I have been a part of your life before that?"

"You have visited my dreams for almost a decade."

"Your dreams?"

"Yes. And I have known since the very first time I saw your face in my mind, that you would be the end of me. Yet, I still sought you." He lifted a hand, brushing one thumb along my open jaw.

"No, Maz, I would never be the end of you. Never."

He moved his thumb, holding it to my lips. "I realize now that the end is inevitable. My end. This quest was never about me. It is, and always has been, about you. I was the tool meant to help you, not the other way around."

I gaped at him. "You don't think I can wield that staff, do you?"

Mazrith dipped his face toward mine. "Reyna, for the love of Odin, will you please stay silent and listen to me?"

I clamped my lips together as he dropped his hand from my face, then took a step back.

"We cannot win, Reyna." He held his hand up as my mouth snapped open again. "Do not argue. I will be exposed to *Yggdrasil* for what I truly am, and my step-mother will rule the Shadow Court. If she is in league with Orm as we suspect, and they form any kind of alliance, they will become an impossibly powerful force.

You were right, Reyna, that I will not rule by fear or force. I believed that would be the only way to keep you safe, but it is not the life you deserve. The truth is that we are bound to a life in hiding from cruel fae with vicious vendettas."

I shook my head, fierce emotion enveloping me. "No," I breathed, but Mazrith kept speaking.

"I will not do that to you. You are a light too bright to be kept in the dark. You are too bold, too tenacious to be hidden away. You do not deserve to spend your life bound to a monster."

"You are no monster, Mazrith."

He gave me a sad smile. "I truly care to hear you say that. But the world will not agree. Value is not in action anymore. Honor is dead."

"No." A sick feeling was washing through me.

"I will free you from our bond. It was created with my mother's magic. And she no longer lives."

My breath caught in my chest, and for a moment I could have sworn my heart stopped beating. "Mazrith, what are you saying?"

His voice dropped almost to a whisper. "My mother said it could be done. And I know how. But Reyna, know this. Though you will not want to look upon me, I will always be there if you need me. Always."

"Maz, you're speaking madness!" Panic was rushing me now, the weird calm that had taken him almost worse than the rage. "You can't have spoken to your mother, she's dead! What is wrong with you?"

"I spoke to her spirit in the church on *Ravensstar*. She would have loved you. And you her," he said softly. "The horses will try to flee, when I am exposed. Rasa belongs to you now, she has made that choice clear. But please, look after Jarl for me."

Tears spilled from eyes. "Mazrith, please. What are you talking about?" My desperate plea went unanswered.

He held up his staff, and shadows began to pour from the skull. My arm raised of its own volition, and the shadows whirled around the mark on my arm.

"Mazrith!"

The tanned color of his skin was fading as I watched, black and white mottling replacing it. The faint white scars spilt and stretched, puckering and glowing gold. The huge wound in the center of his chest radiated light, blistered and black around the edges. It was as though his glamor was being sucked away into the shadows rushing from his staff. My wrist burned, and when I dragged my eyes from him to it, I saw the mark fading.

He was giving up his mother's magic to remove the bond.

The implications of what he was doing smashed into me.

He was giving up. Giving up the whole quest, his home, his people, his magic.

For me. All of it, so that I could be free.

"Mazrith, I want the bond!" The shadows flurried as his sad, resolute eyes widened. I held my wrist high and willed the black mark to return. "I want to be bound to you!"

"Look at me," he said, a tornado of shadow and gold light rushing around us but his voice clear and hard. "You cannot be bound to this.

"I already am! I love you."

The shadows stopped. Tears flowed down my cheeks as I stared into his eyes. Black was creeping across them, but they were still his.

"You can't." His words were raw.

I stepped into him, pressing my hands to his scarred, puckered flesh. "I will do whatever it takes to heal the pain that you have endured. Whatever it takes, Maz. You feel this?" I pushed hard, digging my fingers into his skin. "Does this feel like revulsion or fear to you?" I stood up on my toes, and pressed my lips to his chest, reaching up to his jaw. He was rigid beneath me. I let go of his shoulder, using my hands to pull his head down toward me, gripping his cheeks, forcing him to stare into my face, to see my sincerity. *My love.*

Slowly, he lifted his own hand, running a black finger through the tears still tracking down my cheeks. "You do not cry."

"I cry for you."

"Reyna, I will serve you for the rest of your days, I swear. Bound or not."

"I don't need you to serve me, Maz. I need you to fight. To win. To be everything your mother wanted you to be."

"I live for you. I love you. I have loved you for years." His eyes were bright and fierce, flashes of gold playing across them. "Do you know how hard it has been to fight this? To make you angry, to keep you away? To force you to hate me, so I don't fall to my knees before you and pledge my heart and soul?"

I stared up at the huge warrior prince, the inky black patches on his chalk skin swirling, the blistered scars jagging across his face. "You have been fighting falling to your knees before me?"

"I knew that my love for you would be my end. First, I didn't trust it. I thought it was a trick, thought I could fight my feelings for the copper-haired woman I became desperate to watch in my dreams every night. But then, when you were here... You were more than her. You were fire and gold, in a world of shadow and blood. I realized that I had to fight for a different reason. To keep you alive."

More tears flowed down my cheeks. "Mazrith, you have to keep fighting."

He took my wrist gently, pulling my hand reluctantly from his face. The mark was pale, but still there. "You... You truly want this?"

"Do you?"

"More than life itself."

He had just proven that. Proven that my happiness, my freedom, meant more to him than his own life. "Put it back, Mazrith."

"You are not just saying that because you don't want to look at me like this?"

I grasped the back of his neck and pulled him to me, pressing my lips hard to his. The tension flowed from his body as he pulled me tight, kissing me back as though his life depended on it.

And in a way, it did.

It was more than a kiss. It was a promise. A promise from me that I would never lie to him, that every word I had said was true.

A promise from him that he would fight on, that he would never become the monster he threatened to let win.

The shadows flowed back, swirling around us so fast I thought we might be lifted from the ground. The mark seared on my wrist, and I relished the flash of intense sensation, tightening my arms around Mazrith's neck.

"I love you," I gasped, between feverish kisses, my words lost to his lips. "I love you." The realization was like a drug, taking over every inch of my body and mind.

And he loved me.

It was like nothing I had ever considered, ever dared to hope for. Everything else in the world seemed a million miles away, and not because of desperate passion, like when I had been in his embrace before.

This was more. Deeper. As deep as any emotion could get. He was part of me, his soul entwined with mine, beyond him, there was nothing.

Nothing.

"You feel that?" I gasped, overwhelmed.

"The bond." He pulled back, his eyes wild, his scars receding, the color returning to his skin. "I am yours, for eternity, Reyna."

"And I am yours."

I had never uttered four more powerful words.

CHAPTER 13
MAZRITH

S he loved me.

She wanted me.

She knew what I was, *what I really was,* and she still loved me.

Passion consumed me as she kissed me, so hard I could feel her hunger. Her need.

We were bound. Truly, magically, and soul-deep.

She was mine, and I was hers.

My arms moved to grip her, lifting her easily. She wrapped her legs around mine, squeezing so tight, as though she needed her body even closer to mine than it already was.

I needed her beyond close. I needed to be inside her, needed to claim her, to truly make her mine.

I moved back a few steps, taking my lips from hers and pressing them to her jaw, her neck, down her chest. She pulled at her shirt, her legs tight around my waist, and I stopped moving when my back hit the bark of the tree behind.

I set her down long enough for her to tug feverishly at her trousers, and I barely had time to untie my own before her hands were there, and she was yanking them over my thighs.

She stared at my raging, ready cock a beat, then looked up into my face.

Desire consumed her expression, and with a growl I reached for her, lifting her again.

Her naked skin against my hands sent waves of pulsing need through me, her breasts pressing against my chest as I gripped her backside, lifting her high against me.

"I love you," I said as she wound her hands around my neck, her ankles crossing at the small of my back as I lowered her slowly, stopping with a hiss as my painfully erect cock found her entrance.

She was so wet, and I hadn't touched her.

"I love you. I need you. Make me yours, Mazrith." Her bright eyes were filled with emotion, and I kissed her, hard.

Pressing into her hot, desperate body made the world around me disappear. All I could feel was her, all I could taste was her lips, all I could hear were her moans of need.

As slowly as I could manage, I lowered her, moving deeper, feeling her tighten around me, gauging what she could take. What she needed from me.

"More," she gasped, and I lowered her until there was no more.

Her hands moved into my hair, her teeth nipping at my lips. She was trembling against me.

She was ready.

I lifted her body, sliding her up my full length, and this time the moan was mine, long and desperate against her lips.

"I'm yours, Mazrith. Yours. Take me."

Her words were all I needed, my control shattering.

I pounded into her, and she cried out, loud enough to wake the dead.

My fingers digging into the flesh of her backside, her nails scraping my shoulders, I thrust, over and over, harder and harder, her tightness spasming around me, her cries filling the forest.

"Mine," I gasped, and her lips found mine again.

"Yours," she breathed against me, between feverish kisses and cried of need.

I was made for her, her body sheathing me like it was designed that way, *perfect*.

Pleasure knotted inside me, building with every thrust, her tightening as I filled her, stretched her.

Her hips began to rock hard against me as I thrust, her breaths coming shorter, her cries higher.

"Yes," I told her, allowing myself to fall away, to lose myself in her desire. "Now, my Queen."

Her hands buried in my hair, her head tipped back, and she bucked against me, pressing me as deep into her as she could. A long, gasping cry accompanied spasms of clenching, and then I was filling her with my release, growling into her neck, digging my fingers into her backside.

"Mine."

She was mine. She loved me.

Pounding pleasure washed through me and she collapsed against me, covering my face with kisses, panting for breath.

"Yours. Forever."

CHAPTER 14

REYNA

"You can look inside my head. If you want."

Mazrith's chest stilled beneath my cheek at my words.

The forest floor was more comfortable than I would have guessed, and I had no idea how long we had been lying there.

"Why would you want me to look inside you head?"

I moved, resting my chin on his hard, bare chest, and looked into his eyes. "I want you to believe me. Everything I have told you — I want you to know it is true, to have no doubts at all."

He stared back at me. *"Ástin mín,"* he whispered.

"What does that mean?"

"My love."

Warmth flooded my already sated body. "I like that."

His eyes flashed. "Better than *gildi*? Because I know

you like that too, regardless of what you would have me believe."

"Maybe I don't want you in my head after all."

His teasing smile slipped. "I believe you. I do not need proof. If anything, I wish you could enter *my* head." He dropped my gaze, staring instead at the canopy of leaves overhead. "Then I would be spared the act of telling you all you need to know."

I sat up, and his gaze fell to my bare chest. I gave him a playful bat on the arm. "If you are to spill your secrets, you will not do it ogling my breasts."

He gave me a long look, then sat up too. I made a point of looking between his legs, and he barked a laugh before pulling me tight to him. His thumb ran down my cheek as he stared into my eyes. "If you play with fire, *gildi*, you'll get burned."

"Don't I know it."

He kissed me, and I was more than ready to swing my thigh over him, and slide into his lap, but he stopped me when I began to move.

"No. Please. I need to tell you who, and what, I am."

"I know what you are. Mine."

He growled in satisfaction, then kissed me again, harder. "And you are mine," he spoke against my lips, before pulling away. "And that is why you need to know. I owe it to you."

He rose to his feet, gathering a fur from Jarl's saddlebag and throwing it over me, before settling beside me again. "The king of the Shadow Court was not my father."

I wasn't sure what I had been expecting him to say, but that hadn't been it.

"My mother never loved him. It was a marriage of political convenience."

"Then who is your father?"

"She would never tell me. What I do know is that he was a gold-fae. And babies produced from two different types of fae are not able to choose the magic they wield. I was born with gold-fae magic."

I nodded, my eyes flicking to his still bare chest, the large scar across the wound I knew to be gleaming gold underneath the glamor. I had known he was connected to gold since the start, somewhere deep down.

"My father was furious. It couldn't have been clearer that she had been unfaithful to him, and he couldn't have the world know that. Mother convinced him not to kill me, but to endow me with his own magic, using his mist-staff. But it didn't work." His eyes grew dark, and he dropped my gaze. "That did not stop him trying though. For many, many years."

Bile rose in my throat. "The scars. The mottled skin."

"Yes. A result of my father trying to insert his shadow-magic into my body. In the end, to stop him, my mother began to use her own considerable magic to convince him that I had finally taken on enough of his shadow-magic to be a true shadow-fae. Whether or not

COURT OF SERPENTS AND SECRETS

he believed her, I do not know, but eventually he left me alone."

The memory I had seen of Mazrith as a child hiding behind the berserker axe filled my mind. "Mazrith, I... I'm so sorry."

His eyes flicked to mine. "Pity is not something I receive well. But I thank you for your sincerity."

"It's not pity, Maz." And it wasn't. "It is regret, and anger. Sorrow for a child who was forced through something abhorrent. If your father was still alive, I would want to kill him myself."

"I regret that was not my pleasure," he sighed. "But, he will be gracing the halls of *Hel*, if there is any justice in the world."

"And long may he suffer," I said, pulling the furs tight around myself. "Do you think this mist-staff can do what the King's couldn't, and turn you into a shadow-fae?"

"It does not surprise me that it did not work, his intentions were to harm, to seek retribution."

"Against a defenseless child?" My fists were clenched, and Mazrith reached out, resting a hand over mine.

"He is dead. Our enemies have changed."

We fell silent a minute, and I worked to keep my raging emotions under control. Opting for a change of subject, I spoke.

"Tell me about these dreams."

He raised a brow. "Of you?"

I nodded. "Yes. Years, you said?"

"Yes."

"And what do I do in these dreams?"

"What you always do. Fight." I frowned at him, and he continued. "I would see your interactions with others. Never enough to work out where you were, but enough that I got to know you. Got to feel your determination and spirit. Your passion." He let out a long breath. "Enough to start to fall in love with you. And then, when I finally found you..."

"Maz..."

"You were everything I had seen, and more. A voice of defiance in a world of madness and cruelty." He twirled a lock of my red hair around his finger. "Red, in a sea of brown. Bravery, in a world of cowards."

"I am not brave. I have been terrified my whole life. Running, my whole life. And I only realized I was running from my own head when you pointed it out, mere days ago. There is nothing brave about that."

"Reyna, I watched you offer your own life for your friends the day I brought you here. Do you know how many people would do that?"

"You underestimate humans, Maz. Your world is filled with fae. Greedy, honorless fae. There are many in the human clans who would act as I had. Including Lhoris, and Kara."

I thought he would argue, defend his kind, but he looked at me thoughtfully. "Perhaps you are right. Or, perhaps we are both wrong." He leaned forward and kissed me. "I didn't know if you were sending the dreams on purpose. Not until I met you. And even then, I wasn't sure if you were lying to me."

"So, the night I confessed all to you..."

"Yes. I was waiting for you to admit that you had been inside my dreams."

I shook my head. "I don't know what I am Maz, or who is interested enough in me to send me the visions, but I swear, until coming here I had only had the gold-induced visions of the Starved Ones."

"I know. I believe you."

I nodded, then swallowed and asked the question I now didn't want the answer to. "You said you knew I would be the end of you. What does that mean?"

He cupped my cheek. "I just knew. The trepidation, the intensity, everything about my dreams of you. Danger. Fate. The end. I can't explain it, except that my certainty is soul-deep."

I knew that kind of feeling. I had experienced myself, more than once.

"I thought earlier today that it meant you would be the end of my glamor. This pretend me. That I could sacrifice that for your freedom."

I ran my hand over his chest, along the faint scars. "And now?" I whispered.

"And now, I don't care what it means." He pulled me into him, across his lap, the furs falling away from my chest as I squealed. He pressed his lips to mine, swallowing the sound, and heat flowed deliciously through my body.

I put a hand each side of his head and pulled him back. "Mazrith, I want you to listen to me. I don't care what you look like, or what anybody else thinks of you. I care that you are the person I have spent the last few weeks with, trying to save the world."

He stared into my eyes. "Then, let me be that for you. I recall a dream of yours where you saw the true male inside of me. A side of me that you have yet to experience." The heat intensified as his voice dropped low and husky. "I recall promising to make you beg, *gildi*."

"I will never beg," I told him, desperate for him to prove me wrong. His hand covered my mouth, silencing my words. I squirmed against him, feeling just how hard he was.

He leaned down and then I felt his tongue flick across my nipple. I moaned, my hands twisting around his neck, and he wrapped his hand in my hair, tugging it hard.

He spread my legs with one of his, and his other hand slid down my stomach, stroking.

"Then I will have to make you ache. I will make you crave."

A featherlight touch flicked over my heat and I gasped at the sensation.

His head pulled away from my breasts, his hand left my hair, and he lifted me from his lap, setting me down in the furs.

He slid down my body, kissing me. I watched, breathless, as he reached my spread legs.

I felt his tongue on my clit, felt him flick against me, then his finger against my tight, wet entrance. Slowly, tongue still flicking, he pressed his finger inside me.

I could not hold back the cry, and he froze.

I opened my mouth to protest, to ask for more, but clamped my lips shut.

He looked up at me, a wicked smile on his lips, then dropped his head again.

Another flick of his tongue, then I gasped as his finger thrust and twisted, and I tightened around him.

I whimpered his name involuntarily, and again he froze, the sensations pausing.

I squirmed against him, around him, and he gave a throaty chuckle before his hot, broad tongue began to move against me again, his finger joined by another, curling against me, pressure building fast, as though I could get there before he stopped again. But as I started to clench, focus slipping, the world beginning to tip away, he growled against me. "Beg me. Beg for release or I stop."

I obeyed. I couldn't stop the words from coming. "Please! Please let me come!"

His tongue sped up, his fingers steady, hard, *perfect*, and waves of pleasure washed over me as I came, hard, bucking into him, my body pulsing with desire. He moved quickly, turning me over, onto my stomach. I felt his strong hands on my hips, pulling me up onto my knees. I whimpered as he stroked between my cheeks and pressed against me.

"You want my cock, *gildi*?"

"Yes." He pressed against me, but stayed there, at my entrance. Hard, hot, huge.

"Then hold on to the furs," he told me. "And beg for my cock." Try as I might, I could not stop my hips from wiggling while he teased me, his wet fingertips circling my entrance, flicking against the delicate skin.

His other hand slid up my back, pressing me down. I moaned. It was driving me insane, the feel of him against me, and without meaning to, I thrust against him. He swore, grabbing my hips. I bit my lip, my eyes squeezing shut.

"I will take your pleasure, as many times as I can," he told me, his hands sliding up my back to tangle in my hair, to grip my neck. "But not until you beg. Say please, *gildi*."

"Please," I whispered, my head going light, my body trembling as I felt his cock slide against me. It was slick with my wetness.

"Louder."

"Please," I told him, my voice desperate. He thrust into me, and I cried out his name, my body instantly tightening around him. He held me tightly against him, and I felt him grow even harder, felt him press deeper inside me.

"Again," he said, his voice hard.

"Please," I moaned.

"Please what?" He pulled my hair, pulling me even

tighter to his body, filling me more deeply than I knew was possible.

I pleaded. "Please take me. Make me yours."

His control broke with a snarl, and he thrust into me, a deep, hard, claiming thrust. I gasped, and then cried out as he pulled back and thrust into me again.

"Please," I begged him, my body humming as his rhythm grew faster. My hands twisted in the furs as I pushed back against him, moaning his name.

"Mine," he growled, moving faster, his hands gripping my hips, pounding into me.

"Yours," I agreed, my body clenching around him, and he growled, moving faster, filling me until I thought I might break.

I rocked against him, feeling the intense pleasure build inside me, the heat growing stronger, my mind emptying of everything except the feeling of him dominating my body. I pressed my face into the furs, my eyes tightly closed, and rammed my hips back against him, moaning while he thrust into me. I felt his hand moved between my legs and cried out as he flicked his thumb over my clit.

"Come now, *gildi*. Come for me."

Once more, I obeyed. My body tightened around him, my head going light as I fell, headfirst, over the edge. Pulsing waves of pleasure kept wracking my body and his thrusts slowed but hardened. He scooped one strong arm under my stomach, lifting me so that my back was pressed against his chest, his mouth finding my neck, his hands moving to my tight nipples.

"I love you," he breathed against my skin, and pressed himself into me, his cock pulsing as he found his own release.

And somehow, I tipped again, barely managing to gasp a reply as I saw stars. "I love you too."

CHAPTER 15
MAZRITH

"Reyna, wake up. We must return to the palace before the townsfolk find us here."

She stirred, then rolled over, pressing her face to my chest. Her warm breath tickled as she giggled.

"Not very princely, being caught naked in the forest."

"It's my forest. I'll do what I like in it."

She laughed again, then pushed herself up. "Fates, you're beautiful," I breathed as she stood, gloriously unclothed.

"You just told me we have to leave," she grinned, pushing her hair up and away from her face, then glancing at my already stiffening cock. She began to move toward me, and a flurry of golden runes washed from my entire body. They floated from my face, before my eyes, peeled from my chest, my stomach, even my thighs.

"Oh gods," whispered Reyna, freezing.

I swore too, willing the runes to stop. None had floated from my body whilst we had been together, but now it seemed my magic was making up for it.

"Why would us being together make your mother's magic leave you faster?" Reyna said, her voice soft and sad.

"I don't know. I should have asked her." I got to my feet, the flow of runes now barely a trickle. "But, if we are to continue to fight, then I need what magic I have left. To keep you alive in the *Leikmot*, and to stop my stepmother or Orm trying to seize power if they believe I am weak."

She nodded, her eyes wide. "Maz, I'm sorry. I don't want to be the end of you. In any way. I love you. I don't want to hurt you."

I reached for her, but another rune whisked up from my cheek and I batted it away angrily. "You are not hurting me. But we must form a plan, and act swiftly."

She began to dress, and I followed suit reluctantly. "What was in the flask you had, in the mountain? Could that help make your magic last longer?"

I made myself look at her. "No. That was...a concoction of Tait's. There is none left, even if I was comfortable using it."

She gave me a mildly worried look. "What was it?"

"Regenerative magic that was stolen."

"Stolen from who?"

I sighed. "The Fenrir."

"The lost wolf race?"

I was surprised she had heard of them. "Yes. Tait has a way of extracting some of their magic from relics. It is a questionable practice, and I do not like it at all."

"That claw inside the chest," she said thoughtfully, running her fingers through her hair to try to remove some of the twigs and leaves caught up in it. "That was a wolf claw?"

"Even if it is, there is no time to make more."

"Oh." She looked disappointed.

"I don't suppose you discovered anything useful about the mist-staff while I was..." I trailed off.

"Sulking?" she offered. "No. Nothing. You should try to connect with it again, now that you are not so angry."

I started to argue, but stopped. "Do you have it with you?"

"Of course. I'm not letting it leave my side." As she strapped her belt on, she passed me the simple compacted wooden staff. "Are you, erm, doing this naked?"

"Do you think the staff cares?"

"It would if it had eyes. *Anyone* with eyes would care if you were naked."

"Would you like me to get dressed?"

"Never. I think you should do everything naked. Although I'd need the staff back to fend off every rabid girl or boy who threw themselves at you."

I knew she was teasing me, but the knowledge that she found this form of me so attractive only made the certainty that she would not enjoy my true form worse. My feelings must have shown, because her smile slipped.

"Mazrith, I don't care what you look like, honestly. I'm sorry."

"I know."

I flicked the staff, and it morphed into its full length. I closed my eyes and tried to let my magic flow into the wood. Any magic. Not just my shadows, but any gold magic I had lurking under the glamor.

Nothing happened.

I sighed and handed the staff back to Reyna. "I'm sorry, *ástin min*."

"We'll work something else out. Or I'll have a vision soon that shows us what to do," she said firmly. "You should hold onto it."

"No." I shook my head and thrust it at her. "It would look strange for me to have two staffs. It just looks like an ordinary training staff, it will be much less obvious for you to keep it. And you are right to never let it leave your sight."

She took it, putting into the sheath I had given her, then stared at me. I could see she wanted to move to me as much as I wanted to hold her. "I'll keep it safe. We'll make this work. We have to."

I tugged my trousers on, wishing that we could stay in the glade forever, and dreading the return to the palace and the reality of our situation. I wanted to share in Reyna's optimism, I truly did. But the truth was, we were running out of time, and options.

I would fight, as I promised her I would. But, I would be fighting for her.

CHAPTER 16

REYNA

"My Prince."

Mazrith and I were halfway up the grand staircase of the palace. We both froze at the sound of Rangvald's voice.

Mazrith turned around slowly. "Yes?"

The Queen's advisor dipped his head, his slimy smile not reaching his eyes. "How fortuitous to catch you. I was just on my way to send a messenger to your rooms."

"What do you want, Rangvald?"

"There has been a change in plans for the *Leikmot*. The next round will not be held in the Earth Court, but in the Gold Court instead."

An unwanted shiver ran through me at his words. *The Gold Court.*

I knew I'd have to return at some point, but I hadn't really allowed myself to think too much about what it would be like. Not to mention, the change of location was suspicious.

Mazrith must have agreed, because he narrowed his eyes at the Queen's advisor. "Why?"

"The Earth Court are not ready," Rangvald shrugged. "Something to do with a shortage of human thralls, and otherwise engaged royal family. It is no matter, the Gold Court are already well equipped to hold the next round, apparently."

I wished I could contact Dakkar, find out if it really was the Earth Court who had made the decision to change. But even if I could, it wasn't like we had a choice. I was the *Leikmot* champion for the Shadow Court. I had to go.

"When will it be held?" barked Maz.

"We are leaving at dawn."

"Then I shall leave at noon."

Rangvald lifted a finger. "Ah, actually, Her Majesty wishes you to travel together in convoy. She believes it sends the other courts the right message, to see mother and son traveling together." He gave Mazrith an exceptionally obsequious smile and I managed to stop my lip curling. The male was a weasel. As my brain started to create an image of him with ears and a tail, darkness descended over my eyes.

It cleared fast, and I found myself inside Rangvald's head, looking at Mazrith and I on the stairs.

Fear pounded through him whenever he focused on

the Prince, mingled with a streak of regret. But when he glanced at me, a new emotion swelled. *Guilt*. Furtive, almost panic-stricken guilt.

The vision lifted, and I squeezed the stair banister with sweating hands, trying to keep any evidence of what had just happened from showing on my face.

"I do not wish to travel in convoy," Mazrith was saying loudly. "The Queen made her decision about how to present herself to the other Courts when she kidnapped their loved ones for entertainment. I will not associate with her any more than I am forced to."

"My Prince, you and your—" Mazrith interrupted him with a vicious growl, and he stumbled over his next word "—*stepmother* have walked a fine line for many years now. It would not be wise to upset the balance of things so obviously, not when we are so exposed."

Mazrith strode down a step closer to Rangvald. He backed up instantly. "I am leaving at noon. I do not give a rat's behind when my stepmother leaves."

Rangvald swallowed. "I will pass that on." With the slightest bow of his head, he swept back down the stairs.

"Maz," I hissed as he turned back to me. Concern instantly replaced his angry expression and he reached for my hand.

"Why are you so pale?"

"I was inside his head for a few seconds," I whispered.

Mazrith's eyes widened. "Did you learn anything?"

"It was a spying vision, not a memory. But yes, I think I did. He's scared of you—"

"The male is a coward, of course he is scared of me."

"No," I said, shaking my head. "It's more than that. He's scared of you with a good reason, not just because you are powerful. When he looked at me, he was overcome with guilt."

Mazrith's face hardened. "He is behind the attempts on your life," he murmured. "Come. We must not talk of this here." Still holding my hand, he led me up the rest of the stairs and to the Serpent Suites.

The sitting room was full when we walked in, and every head turned to us as we entered.

"Reyna! We wondered where you had gone!" said Kara, leaping up from where she had been playing a game in front of the fire with Ellisar.

"*You* wondered where she'd gone," muttered Frima, trimming feathers for arrows. "Both of them missing from their beds all night? I had my suspicions that they were perfectly well." She looked up, a knowing smirk on her face.

My cheeks heated, and I was about to come back with a retort, when Lhoris rose from his armchair. "Is it true? What she says?"

Kara paused, halfway across the room.

"What has she said?" I glanced at Frima, who was still smiling.

"I simply told him that you two had to work out what you both wanted, and that things may not be the same when you returned. To be honest, I wasn't sure which way it would go, but..." she shrugged, leaving the sentence unfinished, but looked pointedly at our joined hands.

Lhoris' shoulders tensed. "Reyna?"

I took a breath, and gripped Mazrith's hand tighter. What I wanted to say to Lhoris was that I was in love. That I had found the second half my soul, filled the hole inside me that I hadn't known could only be filled by a hulking, monstrous, beautiful, powerful, loyal shadow-fae prince.

"Mazrith is not our enemy," I said instead. "We all need to work together to stop truly evil folk twisting this world even further from the way the gods meant for us to live."

Lhoris stared at me a beat, then slowly turned and left the room.

I sighed, tipping my head back and closing my eyes.

Kara bounded the rest of the distance between us and I let go of Maz's hand to let her hug me. "He needs time, he'll be fine," she whispered. There was a hint of desperation to her tone, and I looked over her shoulder at Ellisar, sitting with his legs crossed, a huge tankard in one hand and a lopsided grin on his squashed face.

"Are you going to going to join us for lunch?" asked Frima, setting her arrows down. The question was directed at Mazrith.

"Yes. We have plans to make. Reyna needs to win the *Leikmot* if we have any chance of gathering enough support to destroy my psychotic stepmother once and for all. And there's just been a last-minute change we need to discuss."

CHAPTER 17

REYNA

"Come with me," Mazrith said quietly as everyone moved into the war room, ready to eat. He continued past, stopping at the door of his temporary bedroom. I followed him into a much plainer but still nice bedroom. There was a window over the bed at the end, and a door I assumed led to a washroom. The bedsheets were black, and a large wardrobe and full height mirror dominated one wall.

"Are you alright?" Mazrith asked, once the door was shut. He reached out, tipping my chin up toward him. "I do not wish to see you and your mentor at odds. That must be difficult."

I stepped into him, overcome with affection. "Lhoris loves me, he told me that just a few days ago. He's the closest thing I have to a parent. He'll come round. You can help, you know." I leaned back, looking up into his swirling eyes.

"Anything, for you," he whispered.

"Show him how good you are for me. How much you love me."

"I will show you how much I love you every moment I am afforded." He bent, kissing me softly. "But now, we must discuss Rangvald." His chest swelled under my arms, and I released him, sitting on the edge of the bed.

"He is involved, I am sure. But I do not think it is the Queen who has charged him with having me killed."

Mazrith looked thoughtful. "You should call your owl. I am finding him increasingly helpful."

I grinned. "He'll be delighted to hear you say as much," I said. Before I finished the sentence, Voror appeared with a swoop, landing on the pillows.

"I am not delighted. It is obvious and should not have taken him this long to realize it," he said.

"Some of us need warming up," I told him.

"I see you two have *warmed up*."

"Yes. We have resolved our differences." I beamed at Mazrith, my cheeks warm. I was relieved Voror hadn't followed us into the forest. Or maybe he had and was being polite.

"And the matter of the mist-staff?" Voror said.

"We've not worked that out yet. I saw into Rangvald's head earlier, though. I think he is involved with the plot to kill me, because he is terrified of Maz and felt guilty when he looked at me."

Voror tilted his head. "Guilty? That is unlikely, if he

paid an assassin to kill you. That is not the action of somebody remorseful."

I relayed his words to Mazrith, and the Prince nodded. "True. And I think you are right about the Queen. She cannot be involved."

"No. If she knew about the shrine and had the ability to follow you down there, then we would already know about it."

"And Rangvald is her closest advisor. If he knows about it, surely he would have told her," Maz said.

"You know, I don't think he is as loyal to the Queen as you think he is," I said slowly. "He gave me the very distinct impression that killing off all the *shadow-spinners* was a big problem for him. I think he knows just how dangerous she is to the shadow-fae, as well as the rest of *Yggdrasil*."

"But, why would he want you dead?"

"I don't know. He can't be working alone. The snake was put in my room by somebody with access. That could only be done by someone within our circle."

Mazrith shook his head. "No. I trust them all. With my life."

I sighed. "Then somebody is spying on us, and they have a lot of power."

"This is the Shadow Court palace. It is full of powerful spies." Mazrith gave me a dry look. "Although I believe I am in a room with one of the best spies here."

I squirmed uncomfortably. "I am not choosing to spy."

"No. But we must use it to our advantage."

"I wish I could choose when I get the visions," I muttered. "And I want to know why I got none in the Ice Court."

"You are worried you will not get any in the next round of the games?" asked Voror.

"Yes," I admitted. I looked at Mazrith, who was glancing between the owl and me. "You think me winning the *Leikmot* will help you gain power in your Court?"

Mazrith nodded. "Yes. To overthrow the Queen and her mist-staff we would need support. It would help if her own plan to humiliate us went horribly wrong and made her look the fool."

"You winning the *Leikmot* is extremely unlikely," Voror said.

"Well, it'll be even harder with no visions to help. It was hard enough just to survive in the Ice Court, let alone win anything," I sighed.

Mazrith stiffened. "No harm will come to you."

I smiled at him, trying to be reassuring, and lifted my braid. "I know. Look. I'm better than they think I am."

"You are better than all of them" he growled.

"Thanks. But, all the same, I'll take some magical help, if I can get it. Especially if we're headed to the Gold Court next."

Mazrith stood up, his face troubled. "I don't like the last-minute move."

"Me either. But when we were playing kubb, one of

the children mentioned something about a sickness. Perhaps the Earth Court really aren't in a position to host the games."

"Hmm. I think we should be very, very careful."

I gave him a dry look. "You kidnapped me from the Gold Court. I am one of their most valuable assets. And now, you're going to take me back there. You think I wouldn't be careful?"

He took my hand, eyes softening. "I am taking you back as my bound betrothed. Not a Court slave. All shall see that. And if Rangvald is working independently of the Queen and we have more enemies than we thought, then I think we must take Lhoris and Kara with us too. They are leverage on you, and they must stay where I can keep them safe."

His gaze dropped from mine, and I realized what he was struggling to say. "For as long as you *can* keep them safe," I whispered, stroking my thumb over his knuckles.

"Yes. That is the other reason I wish to keep them close. Orm and the Queen may be planning something in the Gold Court, or my magic may run out while we are there. If either of those things happen, we may need to act fast. I know you would never leave them behind if we were forced to run. So, they come. They stay by our side."

Love for him burned through me. "Thank you, Maz. Thank you." I moved to kiss him, but something caught my eye.

"Maz, look!"

My ring was changing. The stone the serpent held in

its mouth was changing color, the color of the gemstone seeping away and gold and black tendrils rushing in, swirling together.

Maz looked from the ring to me, his eyes alive. "It is a firestone. Very rare, and capable of connecting with you." He brushed a finger along my jaw. "You have accepted me."

"I accepted you before now."

A smile took his lips. "Then those feelings have now made their way to your ring."

I held it up, watching the gold and black swirl together in a mesmerizing dance. "Maybe I don't hate it so much anymore." I grinned.

CHAPTER 18
REYNA

L unch was a very different affair from the last few shared meals we had eaten in the Serpent Suites, although Lhoris did not make an appearance.

Everyone was laughing and talking, the awful tension leaking from Maz, or caused by his conspicuous absence, gone completely. Even Svangrior was joining in the banter, though I couldn't help feeling as though he was the only fae in the room I didn't trust completely, despite warming to him in the Ice Court. I couldn't see Frima betraying me, and my friends were an impossibility. So that left Svangrior, Ellisar, or Tait. Of the three, he was significantly wilier and angrier than the other two.

The conversation stayed constant, and most of it was dominated by talk of what the Gold Court might hold for us.

"It will feel very strange for you to go back to the

Gold Court, Reyna," said Kara. "Do you think you will see our old workshop?"

I couldn't tell if there was wistfulness or fear in her tone. "No, I don't think we will be safe to enter the palace at all."

I nudged Maz in the ribs, wanting him to be the one to tell her she was coming too.

"I have decided," said Mazrith, his voice loud enough to carry across the other conversations around the table. "That we will all be going on this trip."

Tait beamed, Kara gaped, and Ellisar banged his tankard on the table. Renewed chatter began.

"But Reyna, what if they try to take us back?" Kara said. "You're a champion in the games, they won't be able to kidnap you, but Lhoris and I..."

"They will not lay a finger on either of you," said Mazrith. He glanced at me, then back at Kara. "Assuming, that is, that you do not wish to return to your workshop in the gold palace?"

I looked sharply at Maz, then his words sank in. I hadn't even considered that my friends might *want* to return to their home.

"But if we leave them in the Gold Court, they could be used against me, by Orm, or other enemies," I blurted. "I can't let them get hurt because of me."

"Reyna, it's okay," said Kara with a smile. "I want to stay with you."

"And Lhoris? Do you think he will want to return?"

"He misses working with gold," she said quietly. "So

123

perhaps. But I think that even if he did, he would stay with us until this is over."

"Whatever *this* is," I muttered. If the Queen took full control of the Shadow Court, then we would be fighting to the death or fleeing. Neither option involved the Gold Court. I sighed. "I will ask Lhoris later. It must be his choice."

Kara looked past me, at Maz. "Thank you." He cocked his head in question. Her voice quavered a little to start with but leveled as she spoke. "For offering to free us. You and your warriors are not what we were led to believe in the Gold Court." She looked at me, then back at him. "You appear to be honorable. All of you."

Maz bowed his head. "I am sorry I took you from your home in the way I did."

"The justification for our kidnapping was more honorable than he can tell you," I said awkwardly. "Honestly."

"I believe you. And I look forward to finding out about your secret quest, once you are victorious." Kara beamed at me, and not for the first time, I wished to the gods I shared her confidence in me.

After lunch, Mazrith and Frima left to oversee the loading of the ship, but not before he caught me alone as everyone else filed out.

"Reyna, I... I wish to tell Frima."

"About us? Trust me, she knows." She had been throwing me grins and knowing glances all through the meal.

"No. About me."

I laid my hand on his arm, warmth spreading through me. Telling my own friends my secrets had not only been easier than I thought, but it had felt so surprisingly good afterward. To not feel so alone, and to know they loved me despite my secrets was like a weight lifted that I didn't know had been trying to sink me. "I think that is a good idea. And, I think she already knows more than you think."

He nodded. "Until we know who is working with Rangvald, it is only her I will tell."

I knew that was in deference to my own distrust of his warriors, and I squeezed his arm in thanks. "I'm sure they are all completely loyal. But—"

"I will take no risks," he said, cutting me off. "The mind is fragile and can be bent to other's wills. I am not so stubborn that I am blind. Only Frima will know."

Svangrior looked annoyed when Maz told him he didn't need his help with the ship, and announced he was needed in the armory anyway. Ellisar went with the moody warrior, and Kara and I played chess. After making absolutely sure that Lhoris was still in his room, I told her as much as was decent about Mazrith and I, leaving out anything that wasn't my secret to tell and wasn't to do with the quest for the mist-staff.

"You had sex on a tree?" Kara mouthed at me, jaw agape.

I blushed as I nodded. "And it was like nothing I even knew was possible."

She shook her head, her own cheeks pink. "I can't even imagine!"

"You may not have to just imagine, if you like Ellisar as much as I think he likes you." I said the words with a teasing lilt, hoping she wouldn't clam up. She didn't, an awkward giggling guffaw escaping her instead.

"He doesn't like me like that."

"Hmm. Do you like him?"

"He's smarter than he looks."

"That's not an answer."

"He's into food, and fighting, and... *sex*." She whispered the last word. "At least, when he talks with the others, that what he says he's into. He doesn't mention those things much to me. Except the food."

I smiled at her. "What does he talk to you about?"

"Medicine. Magic. History."

"Maybe all the fighting and fucking banter is just that. Banter."

"Reyna, I have read about his type." She shook her head. "No. Ellisar and I are not well matched."

"If you say so," I said, then remembered that was exactly what Frima had said to me when I denied any feelings I had for Maz.

126

"I do. So, what happens now with you and Mazrith?"

"I don't really know. We can't be together until..." I tried to come up with something true but vague. "Until his stepmother is dealt with."

"And how is he going to do that?"

"*We* are going to try to win the next round of the *Leikmot*, gather the support of the Shadow Court, then see what happens after that."

"I think the switch to the Gold Court is suspicious," Kara said.

"I know. I agree. But please, don't be worried about coming with us. We will stay away from the palace and Orm, and Maz and his warriors will keep us safe."

"I know. I trust them. But you have to talk to Lhoris. I don't know how he'll feel about going back."

I closed my eyes, then forced myself to my feet. "You're right. And there's no time like the present."

Brynja had bought a cart laden with snacks and drinks to the suites just an hour before, so I took a tray with some of everything on it, and nervously made my way to Lhoris' room.

"I have food for you, Lhoris," I called through the door. "And brandy."

"Enter."

He was smoking his pipe by the window, staring up at the blanket of stars in the sky beyond, and didn't turn when I set the tray down on the desk.

"I can't apologize to you for being with him, Lhoris. It

would be insincere," I said quietly. "But I can tell you that he is not what you think he is."

"This world is not what I thought it was," he answered, just as quietly. "You see that sky?"

"Yes."

"It is beautiful."

I cocked my head. It hadn't been what I'd expected him to say. "Yes."

"I never thought I would see a sky that did not belong the Gold Court."

"I *knew* I would."

He turned to me, his eyes hard. "Yes. You may have the power of gold-giving, but you were never meant for the Gold Court."

Ice trickled through me. Was he rejecting me after all?

His look softened, and he stood, one arm reaching for me. "Do not look so sad, Reyna. It is not you I am angry with."

I took his hand. "You should not be angry with him either. He is not evil, not greedy, not cruel, I swear."

"Reyna, my ire is with the world. With the forces that dragged you into this so utterly unprepared."

"You're not mad at Mazrith?"

"No. I have seen that coming like a boulder down a precipice. I just do not understand the way the gods work. If you are meant for more, then you should have been given time to prepare. Time to become strong enough." Frustration laced his words.

I smiled at him. "That is what I am doing now. What these fae are helping me to do. Prepare. Become strong."

He squeezed my hand tighter. "Strong enough to defend yourself against them?" he whispered.

"Lhoris, I told you. I do not need to defend myself against them. They are not our enemy."

"The Prince, yes. I see that. The way he looks at you... I believe the depth of his feelings."

"He has been looking for me a long time. We are connected, and it goes deeper than reason or sense. It is fate."

For the first time, Lhoris smiled. "Then, I am pleased for you."

"Really?"

"Yes. But it does not mean I trust the rest of them, or this place."

"You just said it was beautiful."

"All the more reason to distrust it."

I bit my lip. "There was an announcement today. The Earth Court is not hosting the next round anymore, so we must all travel to the Gold Court tomorrow."

He stiffened. "All?"

"Yes. We think the last attack on me was not orchestrated by the Queen, so Maz doesn't think it is safe to leave you in the Shadow Court this time. And it is suspicious that the next round has been moved from the Earth Court. He suspects foul play and wants you and Kara with us if we have to react quickly."

Lhoris stared at me a long time. "You know what it

will look like? Him parading his stolen slaves in front of the gold-fae, when they cannot make their staffs without us? He is asking for trouble."

"No. He is taking you purely because you are important to me, and he knows I will not leave you behind in the Shadow Court at the whim of the Queen if..." I trailed off, not wanting to say too much.

"If you have to flee," Lhoris finished for me, on a long sigh of realization. "You think you may end up on the run after all."

"Yes. But unlike when I was fleeing from Orm and the Gold Court, this time I will not be alone. Mazrith will never leave me."

Lhoris reached up, pulling at his beard, his eyes fixed on mine. "Then I will come, without complaint."

"Thank you," I breathed. "And, if we are not forced to flee, Mazrith asked Kara if she wanted to return to the Gold Court when this is over. He will ask you the same."

"We are not his captives anymore?"

"We never were. He took us to keep us safe. When there is no threat, we can live where we like."

Lhoris' look softened. "And you? Will your place be by his side?"

"Yes."

"Here?"

I nodded. "This will be his Court, when his step-mother has been dethroned."

Lhoris looked at the black rune on my wrist. "And you are the Shadow Bound Queen."

CHAPTER 19

REYNA

I didn't see Mazrith again until I was in bed, drifting off to sleep in his enormous four-poster.

He didn't wait for an answer after knocking softly, and my heart swelled when I drowsily focused on his large form entering my room and closing the door behind him.

"Can you stay?" I asked him as he sat down on the bed, reaching out and cupping my cheek.

"You know I can't."

I pulled a face, but didn't argue. "How did it go with Frima?"

"Good. I am glad to have told her. She will fight by my side, whatever comes." I could hear the relief in his voice, and I smiled at him in the low light of the fireplace.

"I knew she would. And so did you, deep down."

Emotion swept across his eyes, and he bent to kiss me. A gold rune floated from his collarbone, and the fire

131

that had begun snaking its way through my veins as his tongue had found mine was doused instantly.

He stiffened, then stood up, his lips a tight line of regret. "Curse this magic," he muttered.

"Goodnight, Maz."

"Goodnight, *ástin min*."

I knew we couldn't risk losing his magic just to be intimate. But that didn't stop me dreaming of him, and of every single intimate thing I knew he could do to me when this was over.

"Odin's raven," I breathed, staring.

It was noon the next day, and our whole party was on the shore of the root-river, carriages loaded with our belongings ready to be transferred to our boat.

The Queen's ship had waited for us, instead of leaving at dawn, and the sight of it took my breath away.

It was terrifying.

The wood had been painted black, and instead of a serpent at the head there was a representation of the awful shadow-beast I had had the misfortune of seeing in action more than once. Set at intervals along the railings were carved heads, many wearing horned helms, expressions of pain or terror on the faces of the wooden victims. What I hoped was red paint oozed down the side, over the railings and down the hull, where holes were regularly punched and shining spear heads waited.

"Reyna, those aren't real, right?" Whispered Kara next to me, staring at the heads.

"No," I said, more confidently than I felt. "They are carved wood."

I turned her, so that we were facing our boat.

It was a scaled-up version of the one we had sailed to the Ice Court, with a very similar serpent at the head, and all the cabins up on the deck and easy to access. The benches and tables we had stowed away on the last boat were fixed to the planks this time, and there were numerous braziers and larger railings, but otherwise, it was identical.

Svangrior and Ellisar were loading weapons on board, and Frima was helping Brynja drag sacks of food under the deck into the storage area in the hull.

"The last boat I was on only had three cabins, but look, we have more now. And more braziers to keep us warm on deck," I pointed.

Kara nodded but began to turn back to the black and red monstrosity beside our boat.

Lhoris marched forward, clasping her arm and walking her toward our boat. "This looks to be a mighty vessel," he said firmly. "Let us make our acquaintance with her."

Gratefully letting Lhoris take charge of Kara, I made my way onto the deck and to Mazrith standing at the prow, staring out at the river.

"Sense anything?" I asked him.

"Starved Ones, you mean?" His voice was quiet, but I

glanced over my shoulder anyway. Everyone was busy, and nobody could hear us.

"Yes."

"No. With my stepmother and that ship in convoy, I would be surprised if we run into any conflict on the journey."

I nodded. "Well, I suppose that's something. Those heads..."

"Do not ask."

I felt sick as I glanced back over at the Queen's ship. She was standing in the middle of the huge deck, wearing a blood-red dress with huge skirts, and waving her staff at the bustle of guards and courtiers scurrying around the boat. "We can't let her win, Maz."

"You have the staff?" he asked, almost inaudibly.

I touched my hip. "Of course."

"Then we have as much chance as the gods have given us." He didn't sound as convinced as I would have liked him to, but at least he hadn't given up. "There are four smaller boats of courtiers following us in the next few hours," he said.

"Four boats of courtiers? She didn't bring that many to the Ice Court."

"No. I believe she has something in the works. We must be wary."

I looked back at her boat just as two crimson sails unfurled from the main mast, the image of a figure stretched out on a torture rack emblazoned on the fabric.

Wary didn't come close to how that crazy gods-cursed Queen made me feel.

"Who is sharing with who?" I asked Frima when the boat pushed away from shore, following the black and red beast sailed by the Queen.

"You're with me. Kara is with Brynja, Svangrior with Maz, and Ellisar with Lhoris and Tait. But we won't be sleeping in the cabins much. I doubt we'll be staying on the boat in the Gold Court."

"No, the palace is inland," I agreed.

Frima looked at me thoughtfully. "Is there anything useful you can tell us about the Gold Court before we get there?"

"Sure. I can tell you the layout of the palace, and the surrounding towns, but given the number of raids your folk have pulled off over the years, I doubt it would be new information to you."

"Tell us anyway."

Once we were all gathered on the deck with either nettle tea or ale, Kara and I told the fae everything we could about the Gold Court that we thought might be helpful. Tait made notes with fascination, asking questions about architecture, meals, and the way the human clans lived in the towns.

"The main problem you will have is the light," I said.

"It's much, much brighter than the Shadow Court, all the time."

"Does it get darker at night?"

"In the same way your Court does, I guess. A bit, but it is never dark."

Svangrior moved suddenly, slapping at his arms in irritation.

"Just ignore her," Mazrith growled, and looked over at the Queen's ship, half a mile further down the river than us but clearly visible.

"I can't," Svangrior snarled. "I can feel her magic all over me like buzzing insects."

"Really?" I said, alarmed.

"Yes," muttered Frima. "We're all blocking it a little. She keeps sending tendrils of mind magic over, sweeping us."

"Why?"

"I guess she wants to know what Maz is up to."

"Can she get into Lhoris or Kara's heads?" I tried to keep any panic from my voice.

"No. She's sending over no more than wisps, and they are simple to block," said Maz.

"And besides, all we know is that you want to win the *Leikmot*," shrugged Kara.

"Hmm." I stood up, restless. "All the same. Maybe we shouldn't talk about anything else just now."

"I wish to see about a solution for the bright light," Tait said, standing too. "I shall report back when we reach *Yggdrasil* in a few hours."

Everybody drifted away from the benches, and I leaned over the railings next to Frima. "It's strange. My whole life I dreamed of escaping the Gold Court and sailing along these rivers. But now, I feel like I've traveled them more than enough."

"Tell me about it. Want to train?"

"Yes. Definitely."

Mazrith strode over, something that might have been a smile on his lips. "Did you say something about training?"

"Yes. There's nothing else to do."

"What did you have in mind?"

"Given that riding is not an option here, archery."

"No more staff work?"

"Frima said I can only do so much damage with a staff against a fae. An arrow is more lethal."

"That is true. Show me."

I thought I might become self-conscious or nervous under Mazrith's watchful gaze, but the opposite happened. Rather than unsettle me, I found him a calming presence. I wanted to impress him, and my aim when Frima launched shadow targets into the air for me to hit was true from the first shot.

Before him, I had no bow and arrow or staff, I had never ridden a horse, I had never earned a braid.

He had made me stronger.

I became so engrossed in the arrows and Frima's

shadowy targets that when I heard a huge splash, I had no idea what had caused it.

"Kara!" Ellisar's voice bellowed across the deck, and I dropped the bow, sprinting to where the huge human bent over the side of the boat. "She fell! I can't swim!"

My heart froze in my chest. Kara was splashing in the water, her head dipping below the surface and her arms flailing. But another splash had caught my attention, and now bile was rising in my throat.

A Starved One was moving toward her from the edge of the root river. It was missing two-thirds of its head, but its arms were surprisingly intact, and it was making slow but steady progress toward the flailing Kara.

"Maz!" I shrieked, starting to pull off my own furs. But I couldn't swim well enough to help her. I would only make things worse. Changing my mind, I moved for my bow.

But before I could take a step, Ellisar had hurled himself over the railing after her.

"What in the name of Odin's arse does he think he's doing?" swore Frima as she skidded to a stop beside me.

She and Mazrith projected shadows from their staffs at the same time and they flew over the railings.

Kara was kicking in the water, barely keeping her head up, all her attention now on the sinking, flailing form of Ellisar a few feet away from her.

"Kick, Elli, kick!" she was spluttering, clearly torn between flailing her arms to keep herself above water and trying to help him. Frima's shadows wrapped around her arms, pulling her from the water. I leaned over, catching her slender shoulders as soon as she was in reach, assisting the shadows in pulling her up.

"I've got her," I gasped as I yanked her over the railings.

"Good. Frima, a little help." Mazrith grunted. I wrapped Kara in my arms, trying to rub her shaking shoulders dry with my own clothes, but she leaned away from me, back over the railings. "Ellisar...!"

Mazrith's shadows wrapped around the Starved One, pinning it where it flailed and thrashed. Frima's shadows wound around Ellisar, keeping him from sinking into the river.

Svangrior arrived, swearing viciously as he leaned over the railings. His shadows erupted from his staff too, and the combined power of both his and Frima's shadows began hauling Ellisar from the water, still kicking and flailing, coughing up water.

I pulled Kara close to me as they levitated the massive man over the railings. As soon as he hit the planks, their shadows swept away to help Maz.

Kara broke from my grip, rushing to Ellisar and dropping to her knees as he heaved. "Kara, you're okay," he choked around his spluttering.

"Why did you jump in after me if you couldn't swim? What were you thinking?"

I wasn't sure he *was* thinking. He'd reacted on pure instinct to save her.

"I... I don't know," Ellisar spluttered.

I turned away from the pair of them, just in time to see the Starved One explode in a burst of black swirling shadows.

The eyes that had watched from the edge of the root had vanished, and my shoulders sagged in relief.

"How did we not sense them?" growled Svangrior.

"We've been busy blocking magic, not looking for it," panted Frima, out of breath.

"It doesn't look like the Queen has had any trouble." Her ship was still sailing on ahead of us, apparently unhindered by undead monsters.

"Kara, how did you fall in? What happened? Did they attack?" Frima fired the questions at Kara, but Ellisar answered.

"We were just talking at the railings, and Kara saw the eyes. She pointed but I told her it was her imagination, and she pointed again, vigorously, and fell."

Her eyes filled with tears. "I'm such a *heimskr*. I'm so sorry."

"No, you wouldn't have got so animated if I had believed you. It was my fault."

"It was nobody's fault. It was an accident. And now, we're all okay. Right?" But when I smiled at Maz, I saw how serious his face was.

"Right," he agreed sternly. "Everyone in their cabins now. Stay inside until we reach the tree."

But I didn't move with everyone else. Nor did he and Frima. Svangrior gave them both a look, but with a snarl, followed Ellisar and Kara into a cabin.

I stepped close to Mazrith, dropping my voice. "What's wrong? Are there more Starved Ones out there? Are we going to have to fight?"

"It's my power," Mazrith said, voice so low I hardly heard him. "I should not have needed help to destroy a Starved One or lift a human from the water."

My mind flicked back to when he had levitated an entire water serpent from the root-river.

Unease rippled through me, the concern on Frima's face compounding it.

"Do you think it's your mother's magic fading?"

"Or a result of him trying to give it up," muttered Frima.

"Your scars..." I lifted a hand to his cheek. I had thought they were more obvious, but I had believed that was because I was more aware of them now. But, as I stared at his skin, I realized they *were* more obvious. Pale white lines stood out on his smooth skin, everywhere.

He hissed out a breath. "Whatever we are going to do to overthrow my stepmother, I fear we must do it sooner, rather than later."

CHAPTER 20

REYNA

It was a few hours later that we reached the trunk of *Yggdrasil*. The staircases up the inside of the trunk had vanished, and as we rounded the serene collection of colossal statues I stared at the waterfall, remembering the last time I had been here. I felt strong hands circle my waist and I leaned back into Mazrith's chest. One of his hands moved, his fingers combing through my hair.

"I am sorry that you saw me here, in the way that you did," he murmured into my ear. "And I'm sorry I pulled you through the water like that afterward. I was just..."

"Desperate to get away? Trust me, I am starting to recognize what running from yourself looks like."

I swiveled to face him, and he looked down at me. A single gold rune floated from his cheek.

"Horseshit," I whispered. "I so want to kiss you." I stepped back, out of his arms.

His eyes filled with resolution and for a second I thought he would stop me. But he let me go, moving his gaze to the Queen's boat, just ahead of us. She had waited for us to catch up at the Shadow Court doors in the trunk of *Yggdrasil*.

"I do not think it will be long now before this comes to a head."

I couldn't help feeling he was right. A tension was building, no longer caused by him and his rage, but in the air, intangible. Bigger than us.

I turned to the statue of Freya and closed my eyes. "Whatever is coming, keep him and my friends safe, please," I prayed.

Images descended over my closed eyelids, and I stumbled, reaching for something to grip. Mazrith caught my hand, but I was barely aware of it.

I was inside the head of a human guard on the Queen's boat, sailing past the statue of Thor.

He was gaping around in awe, the primary feeling coming from him one of overwhelm.

Excitement thrilled through me. I had been desperate for a vision to show us what to do next, and this could be it. What if the guard moved close enough to the Queen that I could hear her, and learn something useful?

As if hearing my wish, the guard turned on the spot, and walked toward the railing where the Queen was standing, talking to Rangvald.

"He has a shadow-spinner on that boat, and I want

him, Rangvald. How much clearer do I need to make myself?"

I felt fear lurch abruptly through the guard and he spun around, revealing the cause. The Queen's shadow beast was prowling the deck, and it had locked its awful eyes on him.

The fear turned fast to terror, and I could feel the guard's limbs freeze as the creature took an agonizingly slow step toward him.

Could it sense me?

"My Queen, your son keeps the shadow-spinner very close to him, it will not be an easy thing to abduct him, nor do I think it will be beneficial. Once we have removed Mazrith from power, we will be able to take Tait."

The beast took another step toward the guard, a low growl coming from its shadowy body.

"I tire of these games. They are not what Orm led me to believe they would be," the Queen snapped.

At the confirmation that she was working with Orm, I gave a gasp of triumph, and somehow, the guard gasped too.

The beast jumped for him, and the vision lifted.

My own reality flowed back into view as I opened my eyes, and a human sounding cry drifted through the tree.

"Oh gods," I stammered, looking over at the Queen's boat. "Oh gods, I think I just got a guard killed."

It took Mazrith's soothing voice and a full glass of brandy to settle my shaking hands.

"You know, this is a good thing. An escalation in your power," said Voror, who had swooped into the cabin I was hiding in.

"What?"

"You said you wanted the guard to move closer to the Queen so you could hear her, and he did."

I stared at the owl, then told Mazrith what he'd said. "You seriously believe that I made him move?"

"It is not beyond the realms of possibility," said Maz.

"Of course it is!" I stood and would have spilled my drink if I'd had any left. "It's one thing to be able to see through another's eyes. It is quite another to control people!" I shook my head hard, trying to dislodge the sick sense of wrong inside me at the thought. "No. No, I can't be capable of that." I cast my eyes skyward, the wooden ceiling of the cabin my only view. "Whoever is sending me this magic, I don't want this much," I said through clenched teeth. "It's wrong."

"It is powerful," said Mazrith quietly.

"It could be the difference between winning and losing the *Leikmot*," said Voror.

"It would be cheating!"

"Do you believe the others cheat when they use their magic?"

"No, but none of them have the power to control other people!"

"The guard was human, yes?"

I stared at him, feeling sick again at the thought that the shadow beast may have killed him because of me. "Yes. So?"

"I wonder if you would be able to control fae," Mazrith mused.

I held my hands up, shaking my head hard. "Enough. We have no evidence at all that I controlled anything. He may have just moved closer to the Queen of his own volition. A coincidence."

"And... the shadow beast?"

My head swam and I sat back down, swallowing bile. "That was not coincidence," I mumbled. "It knew there was a spy on board its boat. I am certain."

"But, the Queen and her beast will not be able to know it was you."

I shook my head once more, then pushed my hair back from my face in frustration. Mazrith's thoughtful expression fled, his eyes widening. Voror clicked his beak, eyes fixed on me.

"What? What is it?" My stomach clenched tight.

"Your ear." Mazrith was staring, and I moved to the tiny mirror over the washbasin, already dreading what I would see.

It was subtle, but there was no denying it. There was a fine point at the tip of my ear.

My fingers felt numb as I touched it, panic flooding my system. "How...? Why...? What is happening to me?"

"Calm down, Reyna," said Mazrith, moving toward

me. I threw my hands up, catching a glimpse of my wild expression in the mirror. Mazrith paused.

"Calm down? That's easy for you to say! You haven't just accidentally gotten somebody killed!"

"He was a Queen's guard," Maz said gently. "Many more will die when this conflict arises and comes to a head."

I pulled my hair over my ears, squeezing my eyes shut. "Lhoris was right."

"What?"

"I'm not ready. He said I wasn't ready, and I'm not. Not for a power like this. Not for..." *Pointed fae ears? Could I really be fae?*

I sucked in air, feeling the panic rise again.

"I need some time alone."

A brief sting of pain flashed across Mazrith's face, but he moved to the door. "Take as much as you need. But I am here when you are ready."

Frima came into the cabin and slept for a few hours, but other than that, I was left alone with my thoughts for the rest of the journey. And Freya only knew, I needed the time to sift through them.

I had become so sure that the gods were sending me the power I was using. But why would they change my ears? Was the very act of them sending me magic turning me fae?

This line of thought, and in fact every other one I

moved along, led me to the question that made my stomach flip and my mouth taste sour.

I was in love with a fae. So why was I still reacting so badly to the idea of being one?

I had all the evidence in front of me that being a fae did not instantly mean one was evil. I had been laboring the point constantly with Lhoris. So why was I struggling so badly with it?

My identity, my true origin, had always been a mystery to me. But processing the idea of being from a different race altogether, a different world... It made no sense. And besides, I was a *gold-giver*. No fae could create staffs.

A slow, sickening realization washed through me. What if that was why I was important? Why I had garnered the attention of those so powerful?

Because I was a fae, *and* a creator of staffs? That would mean... That would mean there was no need for humans anymore. I could be the reason my own kind could be removed from the world.

I took several long breaths. I was overreacting.

Of course I was. Firstly, even if I was a fae and a *gold-giver*, I was one being. That did not mean all humans were redundant. Secondly, I still didn't truly know I was a fae. I resisted touching the tip of my ear for the millionth time. Could the ears have been brought on by the bond with Mazrith, by our coupling?

It seemed unlikely. But, something had triggered the change.

I needed to cling to what Maz and Voror had said about using it to our advantage. If I was going to be given power, I needed to use it for what I knew was good — which was removing Queen Andask from power and stopping Orm from gaining any. *And working out why the Starved Ones were after me.*

Dragging my resolve about me, I repeated a chant out loud.

"Be worthy of the power."

Whoever was sending it to me, there was a reason, and I needed to do what I had told Mazrith to do. Fight, for good. For honor, and valor.

"Be worthy of the power."

I closed my eyes, a prayer slipping through the chant. *Please gods, let me be worthy of the power.*

CHAPTER 21

REYNA

"Reyna, we've almost reached the Gold Court shore." I was surprised to hear the voice on the other side of my cabin door was Lhoris. I hadn't ventured from the cabin since the inside of *Yggdrasil*, but my time alone had run out.

My mentor gave me a tight smile as I stepped out of the cabin. "I didn't think I would return here. Not after everything that has happened," he said.

"Are you pleased to be back?"

Brynja gave me a quick smile as she went into the cabin after me, gathering up anything left behind. "Thanks," I told her, then followed Lhoris to the railings. The entire boat was shrouded in mist, and I could barely see the others moving around on the deck, piling sacks, weapons and huge folded canvases on the planks.

We joined Kara, who was staring out into the fog. "I

am not pleased to be back," Lhoris answered me. "But it is a better journey than last time."

I bumped my shoulder against his. "Everything is different now."

"Now that you and the Prince are in love?" Kara's voice sounded thoughtful as she turned to me.

"Yes. Together, we will do whatever we need to do to keep us safe. I am being given a gift," I said, trying to draw on the decisions I'd come to in the cabin. "By somebody very powerful. I must not waste it. It has been given for a reason."

Lhoris' brows lifted. "To stop the Queen?"

"I think so." *And to save Maz.*

"There is much to come," said Lhoris, moving his gaze back to the fog.

"I don't doubt it."

When I saw the Queen's black ship emerge from the mist, it was moored on a shore of shining sand, the dense forest looming out of the fog beyond.

An envoy of guards had been sent, lining the sand in gleaming gold armor and helping to move the many, many boxes and bags being unloaded from the Queen's colossal warship to large horse-drawn carriages, only just distinguishable in the pale mist.

"Odin's raven, it is so infernally bright," grumbled Svangrior as the boat bumped against the sandy riverbed, and he rolled a large plank of wood over the railings.

"It is even brighter when the fog lifts," I said, but he had already loaded his shoulders with bags and was stamping down the plank, toward a waiting carriage.

Frima, Ellisar and Maz began to unload our things, stacking it all on a large cart on the back of the carriage. All of them had donned their gleaming skull masks. Tait and Brynja joined us, standing at the railings.

"Should we help?" I called.

"No," came the brisk answer.

A warrior in gleaming gold approached, and Mazrith strode to meet him.

"Good day to you, Prince Mazrith," nodded the guard. His eyes flicked to us, up on the boat, then he held out a scroll.

Mazrith flicked it open. "You are dismissed," he told the guard, who gave us one more look, then returned to the much larger group by the Queen's ship.

Mazrith beckoned us down, and we all made our way down the plank and onto the sand.

"A welcome ball will be held tonight, and the first game will be at midday tomorrow," Mazrith said, scanning the parchment.

"Sounds like what we would expect so far," said Frima.

"We have been allocated an area to set up camp in the grounds of the palace."

"Really?" I looked at him, surprised. "They are letting fae from other Courts into the palace grounds?"

"Yes. And the ball tonight will be held in the palace ballroom."

I swallowed. I knew the ballroom well, but never in a million years thought I would be a guest in it, dressed like the fae courtiers, drinking wine, eating fine food, and dancing. That wasn't who I was. *I wasn't one of them.*

My trepidation must have shown, because Mazrith touched my shoulder. "You are not the same female who left this place. Show them that." I nodded, but the uneasy discomfort had already settled in my gut. It was one thing to accept being a fae in a new world, filled with fae who had not yet mistreated me. It was another to slot into the gold-fae world, a world I had detested my whole life.

"We're ready to go, Maz," said Svangrior, forcing my attention back to the beach.

"Good. Everyone in the carriage."

The carriage rolled through the forest, and I found my memories landing on the night we had been dragged through it by the shadow-fae, and my desperation to be rescued by the Gold Court guards.

"It is no surprise that the Gold Court Queen hasn't come to meet her sister," grunted Svangrior.

ELIZA RAINE

"No," I said. "She would spend large amounts of most royal addresses warning her people of the dangers of the shadow-fae and particularly, her sister and her stepson." I glanced at Maz. "Does Queen Andask ever speak of her?"

"No. Though her eyes get a little more unhinged when her sister is mentioned in passing."

"Why did either of them allow this to go ahead if they hate each other?"

Nobody had an answer.

"I wonder if Orm has more sway than I thought," I mused.

"I had heard rumors of such." Everyone turned to look at Lhoris. The single sentence was the most he had engaged with the shadow-fae, ever.

"You did?"

"Yes. For six months or so before this all started, I had overheard a number of nobles either plotting to cut his influence, or to ingratiate themselves with him. I had assumed he was moving closer to the Queen, but then when he announced he was taking a new bound concubine—" A growl rumbled from Mazrith, and Lhoris gave him long look before continuing. "I wondered if something else was afoot."

"When did you last see the Queen?" asked Kara.

Lhoris looked thoughtful. "At her last public address."

"Which was?"

"Nine months ago." I stilled. I had not seen her in the palace since then either.

"We did notice a distinct lack of gold-fae guarding the palace the night you raided it, looking for us," I said slowly.

"Looking for *you*," Mazrith corrected. Svangrior snorted.

"As I told you then, it is because gold-fae are weak-minded and cowardly," the warrior spat.

I stopped myself from looking at Maz. *A secret gold-fae hybrid*. Did comments like that sting him?

"You believe they are cowards because they are your enemy, but trust me, when there have been attacks before, the gold-fae have defended their wealth. They are not cowardly when it comes to greed." I looked out at the forest, the mist clearing and the bright sky starting to shine through. "There was not enough resistance that night."

Mazrith nodded slowly. "You think something may be orchestrated from within the Gold Court?"

"Perhaps."

"Who would rule the Gold Court if anything happened to the Queen?"

"Her son," said Kara. "But he is very young, only thirteen or fourteen. And besides, the Queen is a powerful fae with loyal guards, it would be no easy feat to usurp her."

"Many a royal fae has been removed from power by nefarious means," said Maz darkly.

The carriage moved up the path out of the forest, over the crossroads, and toward the Gold Court palace.

The light got brighter and brighter, until the reflection off the gold and white castle was making my eyes water, even inside the carriage. I hadn't spent long in the Shadow Court compared with the others, so I could only imagine how uncomfortable the shadow-fae would be.

When the carriage pulled to a stop, we were in a large courtyard on the third level of the palace grounds, the huge fountain I used to swim in right in the center.

We climbed out and I saw the Queen and her enormous entourage setting up tents and trestle tables in the area on the left side of the fountain, closest to the grand stairs that led to the main gates of the palace.

Mazrith looked around, and I could see how narrowed his eyes were behind his mask. "There. That large beech tree. We will make camp there."

"When you took me from the palace the light in the Gold Court dimmed. The rumor was that only you or your stepmother could do that," I said. "Why is the sky not dimming now, with you both here?"

Mazrith gave me a dark look from behind his mask. "My stepmother's power, bolstered by her staff, can do it, and mine at its strongest could achieve it for short periods. But, I doubt it would be the polite thing to do during a supposedly friendly games festival."

"Curse Thor, this is intolerable," muttered Tait as he climbed out beside me, seemingly to himself. "I'm not sure if it will work but we must try. My Prince?"

Mazrith turned to Tait as the warriors began to unload the cart, swearing about the brightness the whole time. "Try what?"

"I believe I can fashion us some eye protection, but I will need some very specific gauze." He looked at me. "Do you know where we could source materials such as fabric?"

"Upper Krossa is a short walk down the hill, and it's the richest town in the Court. There are many tailors and seamstresses, and a busy market. I'd say you could find gauze."

Tait pulled a book from his bag, flipping through the pages, then turned it to face me. "This one."

I nodded, and Maz looked at the carriage. "Frima?"

She came over, eyes streaming under her mask. "Tell me it gets darker than this?" She was looking at me.

"Sorry. Not really."

"Frima, Tait thinks he can help us, but we need to go and find some fabric. Stay here, do not let the humans out of your sight, even for a moment. That includes you," he said, turning to Tait.

"My Prince, much as I long to explore, I will concentrate on eye coverings, and the sphere," he said.

"Good. Because the Queen has designs on you."

"What?"

"Reyna overheard her telling Rangvald that she wishes to increase her number of shadow-spinners. I mean it Tait, stay here, and stay safe. Go nowhere near the Queen's camp, and keep Frima or Svangrior or Ellisar in sight at all times."

Tait bowed his head. "Understood, My Prince."

CHAPTER 22
REYNA

"I never thought to walk through the streets of my enemy's realm so freely," Mazrith said, staring around at the buildings of Upper Krossa.

"And I never thought to be walking them with the fae Prince of the Shadow Court." *My betrothed.*

I resisted the urge to grab his hand.

Part of me had worried that with his power waning, us being alone and so exposed in the Gold Court would be dangerous. But I had taken one look at his hulking form when he had donned all his furs and weapons, his fierce skull mask firmly in place, and ceased worrying.

"Why did you want to come with me yourself?"

He looked sideways at me. "I like being alone with you. And I wanted to see the town."

I wondered if there was another reason. "I'm sorry about last night." I knew he didn't need the apology, but I wanted to make it all the same.

"I understand. But I wish you would let me help you, as you have tried to help me."

"Maz, I was upset about the possibility of being a fae and my ears changing shape. It would hardly be kind, *or fair*, to moan to you — a fae trying to stop his whole body from changing."

Darkness floated across his irises. "I see your point. But pain or confusion is relative. The size of my problems do not diminish your own."

"Oh, Mazrith. You know, you may be as wise as you are hulking."

I saw his eyes narrow at the corners, a result of a smile, I hoped. "You think I could give your wise owl a good competition?"

I laughed. "Never. Why did you want to see the town?"

"I have seen it in my dreams many times. Whenever I saw you."

"Really?"

"Yes. I never saw you in the gold palace, or I would have known where to find you. I always saw you inside buildings, in a town that could be anywhere."

"Huh. Well, Upper Krossa is a big town, with lots of buildings. I rarely ventured further."

I stopped outside a gleaming white-stone building with a pair of scissors carved into the doorway.

As soon as we entered, the occupants fell silent. Two women working on swaths of white fabric, had been chatting animatedly until they saw Mazrith fold himself inside the room.

He blinked around, presumably appreciating the brief respite from the glittering outside.

I smiled at the seamstresses, both brown-haired and plump. "Good day. We're looking for some woven gauze."

"Of course..." The woman looked me over, clearly trying to work out what to call me.

"My Lady," said Maz, at the same time I said, "Reyna."

"My Lady," the woman said, standing from her stool quickly enough to knock it over. Her eyes raked over my hair, and I felt a bristling of defensiveness before she moved on to Maz. "How much do you need?"

"Three yards, please."

She hurried over to the piles of fabrics, and moved to a series of sheer ones hanging neatly on racks. "Color?" she called.

"Black."

She cut the fabric, her eyes repeatedly flicking to my hair. I lifted a lock of it and twirled it. "Everyone is always so thrown by my hair," I said quietly to Maz. He didn't answer for a second, but when he did his words surprised me.

"She is impressed by your hair."

"What?" As she came over to me, the gauze folded neatly, I spoke. "You seem interested in my hair."

She blushed. "I'm sorry to stare, my Lady. But it is so beautiful."

"Beautiful? When I was a thrall it made me a freak, but as a Lady it is beautiful?"

The woman's face changed, her expression alarmed as she looked between me and Maz. "I'm sorry, my Lady, I meant no offense, and I certainly wouldn't have called you a freak, thrall or not."

Immediately regretting my outburst words, I smiled. "No offense taken. I'm sorry. I've just never had my hair complimented before."

"Really? But what a wonder to have shining copper curls as you do! I have a dress here that would make it sing."

"You... You do?"

"I can't sell it here, it is black, and the gold-fae so rarely wear black. But on you, with the red... It would look positively regal."

"I will wait outside while you inspect this dress," said Maz.

"But I don't have any money."

He gave me a look, then produced a coin purse from one of his pouches.

"Brynja has many dresses for me. I don't need another one."

"They were chosen by someone else." His voice was low and intense, his eyes dark behind the mask. "You need to choose your own armor this time. You need to show the Gold Court that you have become more than they ever let you be."

I stared at him. "You think a dress can do that?"

"I remember you in that dress at that first ball, Reyna. I saw you change, saw the glimpse of the real you."

And I remembered his words that night as thought they were burned into my skull.

"I see it in you. You were born for more than your life has offered you. And you know it."

"The dress showed you the real me?"

"You wore it like armor." His voice dropped to a growl. "And you looked good enough to devour."

I stared at him a moment longer, then turned to the seamstress. "I'd like to see the dress, please."

"'That took longer than I thought it would." Mazrith said.

"You and me both," I answered, stepping out of the seamstress's building. "But I hope you'll think the wait was worth it."

"From the smile on your face, I have already decided it is."

I beamed at him, and a shout made me turn. The tavern was only three buildings down, on the other side of the path. A large human was launching a much smaller human out of the doors, roaring with laughter when the skinny man skidded across the sandy ground.

"Hmm. So despite this infernally bright sky, and this accursedly white stone everything is built from, I see the human clans from both the Shadow Court and the Gold Court have much in common," Mazrith muttered.

"Drink, fight, fuck," I answered, squinting at the large man. "Wait a minute. That's Skegin."

"Skegin?" Mazrith's tone was sharp.

"I used to play him at chess, for money. He was adamant that I could never earn a braid because I'm a freak. So I tried to get him to make a bet with me that I would earn a braid before he did."

"Did he take the wager?"

"Sadly, no."

Mazrith squared his shoulders, watching Skegin enter the tavern.

Skegin paused, then spun around sharply. His eyes landed on me and Mazrith.

"Did you do that?" I whispered at Maz.

"His mind is weak."

"He's good at chess. And not a coward."

"He *is* a coward," Maz said. "He fears that which he does not understand."

Skegin's eyes took on a panicked look, and I slapped Maz's arm. "Stop it! I'll deal with this."

I sauntered toward the tavern doors, smiling at Skegin. Maz stayed where he was.

"Good day, Skegin."

His eyes raked over my face, flicking constantly towards Mazrith's huge form beyond me. He was clearly trying to decide whether or not I was a threat. "You are with the Shadow Prince? The rumors are true?"

"He kidnapped me from the palace and made me his bound betrothed. And then I was forced to be the Shadow Court champion in the games festival." I kept my voice as indifferent as possible.

"No. No, that can't be true. What would a fae Prince want with you?" He straightened, his fear seeping away. "That is one of your freaky friends, dressed up."

I smiled. "You believe whatever you want to believe, Skegin. Either way, I earned this, winning a game against three of the strongest fae in *Yggdrasil*."

I lifted my braid, wiggling it at him.

His jaw dropped as he stared at it. "You'll be punished for that!" he spluttered. "You know the penalty for taking braids when they're not earned?!"

"Hundreds of fae and humans alike saw me earn it, Skegin." I roved my eyes over his own mop of hair. "Where's yours?"

His face twisted. "Even if you're not a lying piece of shit and you *did* earn it, one braid doesn't make your hair any less *wrong*. Or you any less of a freak. You're not welcome here."

His words no longer stung, I realized, and a new kind of smile took my lips.

There was no guilt, no pain.

I *didn't* fit in Skegin's world, in any way, shape or form.

And that was okay. I was never meant to fit in here. I

knew where my home was now, and it was wherever Mazrith was.

"You know, Skegin, compared with you and your friends, I am a freak," I smiled at him. "And thank Freya for that."

CHAPTER 23

REYNA

The Queen's camp was thriving with activity when we returned to the courtyard, huge tents both round and triangular dotting the area she had dominated, and scores of campfires burning.

We gave her camp a wide berth as we climbed the gleaming white steps, turning right to the beech tree Maz had chosen.

Our own camp was looking pretty lively too. Six large round tents were set up around one central campfire, which was lit and had a large iron pot hanging over it. Only Brynja and Tait were sitting outside. Both Frima and Svangrior were tucked into the openings of their tents, in an effort to stay in some shade I guessed.

Tait leaped to his feet when he saw us. "I did it! My Prince, I did it!"

He was waving something in his hand that reflected the light, and made us both turn away, squinting.

"Did what?" Mazrith barked, pushing the shadow-spinner's arm down so the shiny object wasn't glaring.

"I worked out how to get into the Ice Court sphere!"

Relief that it wasn't a trap and he appeared fine was quickly replaced with curiosity.

"What was in it?"

"This," he beamed, holding the item up again. I shielded my eyes and peered at it, as Mazrith gave another groan of annoyance.

It was a thin disc of glass, or ice, I wasn't sure which, set in a silver ring with a handle, about the size of my palm.

I looked at him questioningly.

"A truth glass," he said, bouncing on the balls of his feet. "Very rare, made from a substance only found in the Ice Court."

I looked again and saw the streaks of glittering blue in the bright golden light. It somehow looked like it would be cold to touch, and I had no problem at all believing it was enchanted ice.

"What does it do?" asked Mazrith, eyes narrowed as he looked down at it.

"Reveals the truth! You can lay it over script or places where something might be hidden, and it will reveal their secrets."

I blinked at him. "So, if I had a riddle written down, and I laid that over it..."

"The answer would be given to you!"

I turned to Maz. "Well, that would have saved us some time," I muttered.

"I will write down the last one, and we can try it out."

Tait looked at him with interest. "Oh yes, we shall try it on everything! I have many texts in the library that I can't wait to experiment with."

"In the meantime," Mazrith said, and thrust out his hand.

"Of course! Gauze!" Tait took the fabric with a beaming grin, then scurried inside one of the tents.

"Do you think this *truth glass* might help us?"

Mazrith shook his head, glancing around to ensure nobody was listening to us. "No. I don't think the statue gave us a riddle that is hiding a secret. I think the rhyme simply makes it clear that the staff will only respond to one worthy."

I nodded, inclined to agree. "So. Which tent am I taking my new dress to?"

"This one is yours and Frima's." Mazrith pointed at the tent we were standing right next to. It was made of thick, darkened animal hides, intricate knots and woven braids lining the edges of the entrance flaps, and sturdy wooden poles, carved with images of snarling beasts, supporting the sturdy structure. The front of the tent was adorned with a finely stitched raven banner.

I went inside, into a spacious circular room. The floor was covered in thick layered pelts and furs to provide insulation against the cold ground, and in the center, a small firepit provided warmth, the smoke escaping through a hole in the roof.

Along the sides were wooden furnishings, including two handsomely carved beds covered in blankets and pillows. A large oak table stood ready to receive food and drink and weapons, bags and armor were all neatly arranged around the edges, ready for use.

"This is amazing," I gaped.

"Fit for a Queen."

Frima entered the tent right after Maz left, along with Brynja, to get ready for the ball. We ate some cheese and bread, drank some nettle wine, and took our time with the elaborate outfits and hairstyles.

Voror flew in but stayed relatively quiet, only sharing a few comments on the inanity of human and fae culture.

"Where's all the moaning about hating balls?" Frima asked me as Brynja set more powder on my cheeks. "I thought parading around with pompous fae was your idea of a bad time?"

I shrugged at her in the mirror, smiling. "I chose my own dress and partner, this time."

"Gods, you are nauseating." But she was smiling as she said it.

"Do you have a partner tonight?"

She scowled at me as she applied a kohl to her already dark eyes. "Partner?"

"Henrik. I assume he is here." I gave her a look. "Do not bring him back to this tent if you're going to make a noise all night."

Frima snorted. "I assumed you would be sleeping in Mazrith's tent tonight — he's the only one of us with one to himself."

My shoulders sagged inside the robe I was wearing. "We can't be together yet."

"What? You look pretty *together* to me."

"No, I mean... physically."

"Why not?"

Brynja had paused in her application of a red cream to my lips and was looking at me questioningly too.

"It's erm... a distraction we can't afford right now," I said lamely.

"Hmm," said Frima, hopefully understanding that I couldn't give her the truth with someone else present. "Well, *I* won't be bringing anyone back here tonight. I want to stay alert, and ready. Something is off here."

I looked at Brynja. "Is it strange for you to be back? Do you sense anything is different?"

She gave the tiniest shrug of her shoulders. "It is strange to be back, yes. I'd forgotten just how bright it is. I sense nothing different. But I haven't been anywhere but the camp."

"Where did your clan live?"

"By the coast. Nowhere near the palace. Now, for your hair, I thought we could—"

The realization hit me a second too late.

"Wait, no—!"

Brynja gasped, dropping the pile of my hair she had just lifted high on my head, her hands flying to her mouth.

Frima turned sharply. "What is it?"

Brynja was staring at my now-covered ears.

I scrabbled for an explanation, but what could I say? I let out a long sigh. "My ears have changed. Recently."

Frima stood up, frowning. "What?"

With a long breath, and my heart pounding, I lifted my hair to expose my ear.

"Odin's raven, how has that happened?"

"Do you... Do you have... *magic*?" Brynja whispered the last word. "Have you always been a fae? How can you be a fae *and* a gold-giver?" The questions began to tumble from her lips, and I shook my hands.

"No, it's nothing, I don't know how it has happened," I said. I stood and turned to face her. "I'm human, Brynja."

"You sure about that?" asked Frima, cocking her head.

I wasn't about to talk about my visions in front of Brynja, so I just shook my head. "Please, can we just do my hair so nobody can see my ears, make sure my head-band and Voror's feather is included, and forget about it?"

Brynja nodded slowly, but I noticed the trembling in her hands when she went back to work on my red curls.

Everybody was sitting around the campfire when we emerged from the tent, all but Kara and Lhoris wearing strips of gauze tied carefully around their eyes with a series of small metal rings holding the fabric in place. It looked odd, but I assumed it helped them see better.

"Freya's fields, look at you," gasped Kara when she saw us.

Every head turned. Lhoris froze, but Maz slowly got to his feet and pulled the gauze from his eyes.

"You were right. The wait was worth it."

"You look good, too," I told him, feeling my cheeks warm at the sheer intensity of his gaze.

He was wearing his dark shirt and tight trousers, his amulets nestled in the exposed 'v' of his chest. His braids were pushed back from his face with a simple silver circlet with serpents wrapping around it.

"Do a twirl!" said Kara, clapping her hands together and making me drag my eyes from the seven feet of muscle and desire staring at me like I was his favorite fine wine.

"Oh, erm, sure."

I did, and a small thrill ran through me at the way the dress moved, the full skirts flowing out, catching the air and sparkling in the light. The bodice of the dress was black, as the seamstress had said, and it plunged down to the waistline at both the front and back. The full skirts changed from black at the top to glittering gold at the bottom, in an ombre effect, as though the material had been dipped in liquid.

"You think the gold-fae will stay off my back in this?"

"Stay off your back? They'll be all over you. You look like one of them," said Lhoris shortly.

Grateful that he couldn't see my ears, I gave him a look. "That's the idea. I need them to respect me, so that Maz can get followers."

"Nobody will be leaving you alone in that dress," growled Maz as he came to stand beside me. "Including me."

CHAPTER 24

REYNA

Fae from all over *Yggdrasil* were making their
way up the grand central steps up to the palace
entrance, but we still drew glances as we fell
into step with them.

This was the first ball I had attended that had not
been a masked ball, and not just the females wore
powders and colored creams on their faces. A lot of the
men were made up too, and the effect was beautiful.
Everywhere I looked in the gleaming, glittering light
were gleaming, glittering fae. Even the shadow-fae from
the Queen's contingent seemed to have a sparkle in their
black and burgundy outfits.

I knew the palace well, though I had rarely entered
through the front entrance, but it was strange being
back. I had become used to the black and white checker-
board tiles of the shadow palace, and the intricate, gold-
inlaid marble floor looked wrong somehow.

We followed the reams of guests through the entrance hall, towering golden arches stretching high above us, until we reached the ballroom.

I couldn't help a little gasp of appreciation.

The ballroom glowed with a warm, honey-hued light that radiated from the walls. Tall pillars sculpted from shimmering gold stretched up to meet the dazzling crystal chandeliers, runes floating from the metal before my eyes. The marble dance floor swirled with amber and gold as if lit from within, and as couples danced and spun gracefully, trails of glittering dust flowed behind them, as though they'd disturbed the light the shining floor was creating.

Along one wall, a massive harp made of glistening light played a mesmerizing melody, its luminous strings plucked in perfect harmony by a small human lady. Small round tables stood around the edge of the ballroom, covered in gleaming golden platters piled high with treats and delicacies.

"Ellisar would go mad for all that fine food," Frima muttered.

Svangrior was not with us, as he had joined Ellisar in his task of guarding Kara and Lhoris. It was not just the gold-givers that were at risk — we now knew Tait was on the Queen's list of desirables too. I agreed whole-heartedly with Mazrith that two guards, one with shadow magic, were needed to protect all of the rune-marked.

Frima swished the bottom of her skirt, a slinky black

design with a long split that would allow for easy movement and a high halter collar that kept her usually more exposed chest tightly under wraps. "I feel underdressed," she said. The fae really had gone all out with the outfits. Ice-fae were wearing white and blue sparkling dresses made from feathers, earth-fae were wearing green gowns that looked as though they could be fashioned from real leaves, and the gold fae were head-to-foot glittering magnificence.

"You look amazing," I told her.

She gave me a grin as we filed into the ballroom. "I know I do. But I could have gone further. You know, you're getting your fair share of attention."

I swallowed. She was right. My dress was eye-catching, and the black set off my copper hair so vividly, and there was little other red in the room — apart from Queen Andask.

She was easy to spot in the crowd, her burgundy dress so enormous that nobody could stand closer than a few feet to her. The bodice was extremely low cut and edged with rubies that glittered in the warm light, and matched a massive ruby at her throat. Her black hair was piled high on her head and she wore a crown adorned with silver skulls and clear diamonds. There could be no question; she wanted everybody to see that she was royalty.

Her eyes were locked on her sister, sitting on the throne at the head of the room, resolutely ignoring her and staring out at the crowd with a blank smile.

I frowned as I watched the Gold Court Queen. Her son was in a smaller throne beside her, gold inlaid designs of gems and vines etched into the white stone and an arch of intertwining gold and diamonds rising over the back of the seat like a halo. He was leaning over regularly to talk to her, but she didn't seem to be responding.

A thrall in simple white robes approached us with a tray of sparkling wines. We all took one, and I stared around the room.

"Where's Orm?" muttered Frima.

None of us could find him in the crowd. "That's not right. He should be here," I said. "And is it me, or does the Queen look strange too? Her expression I mean." To look at, she looked exactly like a fae Queen — a wealthy one at that. Her hair was long and white, straight as a poker falling down her chest over her pale skin. She wore a demure dress in shape, but not an inch of the fabric wasn't covered in tiny glittering gold crystals. Her crown was throwing up so many gold runes that I couldn't make it out clearly.

"Perhaps we should perform our royal duty," Maz said, indicating the line of guests waiting to express well-wishes to the royal host.

My brows shot up. "You want to go and speak to her? Are you crazy? You stole me from her Court, Maz. Not just me, but three of the eight palace gold-givers! And you want to go and stand in front of her and say hi?"

He looked at me a moment, then her, and nodded. "Yes."

"No, that is a terrible idea." He strode toward the line alone. "*Heimskr*," I snarled, and moved quickly to join him. As I reached him, a gong sounded, and a voice boomed through the room.

"The Queen of the Gold Court welcomes her guests and bids that they enjoy the dancing and food. The *Leikmot* will commence at midday tomorrow, so drink and be merry, one and all!"

The line in front of us began to move as simpering fae kissed the hand of the Queen and her son.

Anxiety gripped me. The Queen wasn't as powerful as her crazy sister — she didn't have a mist-staff — but she was powerful enough that she might be able to best Maz in his current state. Goading her with what Maz had stolen was a really, really bad idea, I was sure of it.

"This is stupid," I whispered. "You said we'd stay out of the way of trouble, and this is inviting it!"

"*Gildi*, you will be up in front of her as part of the festival tomorrow. You can't keep your head down, so we may as well prove that we are not afraid."

"What if I am afraid? She's a fae Queen, Maz!" I hissed the words, ensuring nobody was close enough to hear us. But folk usually gave Maz a wide berth, and this was no exception.

"You should fear nobody, *ástin mín*. Not while I stand beside you."

I stared into his eyes a moment, then I squared my shoulders. "Fine. Let's get this over with."

But when we finally stood in front of the Queen, I wasn't even sure she recognized me.

If she had been following the *Leikmot,* then she must have known who I was, and even if she hadn't I would have expected her to know I was a gold-giver. After all, I had worked on her staff a few years ago. But she held her hand out for me to kiss without a flicker of interest. "Welcome, and enjoy," she said, her voice lilting, but lacking any depth.

I bent my head to kiss the back of her gloved hand and forced myself to make eye contact with her. But her eyes were vacant, I could see no focus in them at all.

I stepped along so that Maz could take his turn. "Good evening," she said to him mildly. "Welcome and enjoy."

"Reyna Thorvald."

I snapped my attention to the young Prince. "Oh, apologies, your highness," I said, curtseying. *His* eyes were far from vacant. In fact, they were darting everywhere, over my shoulder, left and right, constantly.

"You are providing healthy entertainment in the *Leikmot.*" His sharp eyes fixed on mine for a second. "I wish you well."

Really? The Prince of the Gold Court wished me well? Now, that made no sense at all.

I was moved along before I could respond, and heard

him giving Maz a perfunctorily formal greeting as I moved away from the dais.

Maz held his arm out for me a moment later when he reached me, and I gripped it as we strode away from the royals, back to where Frima was waiting for us.

"How did it go? It didn't look awkward from here," she said when we reached her.

"That's because she's too far gone to be awkward about anything," Mazrith said quietly.

"Too far gone? What do you mean?"

"It was like she didn't really know who we were, or what was happening. She was just going through the motions," I said. "And her son, he seemed kind of scared. He wished me well."

Frima frowned at me. "Wished you well? I thought they would threaten you, promise revenge, even take a swipe," she said.

"They should have. Something is very wrong. Where the fates is Orm?" muttered Mazrith, looking around. "He is at the heart of this, he must be."

"You think he's controlling them somehow?"

"I don't know, but the boy was definitely frightened."

"Did you get in his head?"

"No, it was protected. They both were."

"Protected by what? I thought only shadow-fae could do that?"

"No, there are trinkets and such that can do it too, and they are both laden with jewelry. I imagine something on their person will be the cause."

"My son." The sickly-sweet voice of the Queen reached us just as the fae around us parted to let her huge dress sweep through. She smiled, her black teeth making my skin crawl.

"I am not your son," Maz said.

Her smile was replaced by a frown as she peered at his face. "These scars, child. Why have I not seen them before?"

My stomach turned over, and Mazrith seemed to grow and solidify before me. His hand moved to his staff at his hip. "What do you want?"

"I am merely being polite. Is it so strange to speak with one's own family?"

Her eyes flicked to mine, and pain sheared through my skull. I gasped, squeezing my glass too tight and spilling my drink.

Razor blades were raking at my head, and the headband, concealed inside the rolls of my hair, suddenly felt as though it were on fire.

Mazrith gave a bark of anger and stepped forward, but I felt a burst of energy come from within my own head, a feeling like cool running water.

With a swoosh that made me dizzy, the pain and blades vanished.

Queen Andask stared at me, her eyes filled with hatred. "You have found a way to give her your magic," she hissed.

Mazrith looked at me for the briefest second, then

stepped toward her, his boots crushing the burgundy velvet of her dress.

"Touch her again, and I will rip the heart from your chest and feed it to one of your creatures."

"I didn't lay a finger on her, boy."

"And I won't need to lay one on you to carry out my promise."

Her own hand moved to a diamond-encrusted sheath at her side, the tip of her staff gleaming. "Soon, whatever you are scheming will not matter," she said quietly, but Rangvald appeared at her side, his pale face flushed, speaking before she could continue.

"My Queen, I—"

She turned to him, her expression abruptly livid, and swiped her hand out, landing the back of it across his face. She caught his pronounced cheekbone with the huge gem on one of her rings, and blood trickled down his face from the cut it had caused.

I forced myself to stay put as the Queen licked her lips, watching her advisor bleed. Rangvald's eyes filled with hate, but his mouth stayed firmly shut.

"Where have you been?" she said, her voice sing song. The fae around her were staring, but I couldn't see revulsion on their faces, more...intrigue.

"Apologies, My Queen," Rangvald said, bowing his head.

"You may make it up to me now." Her eyes still fixed on the cut on his cheek, she began to walk away. He followed her as though on an invisible leash.

I took a long drink from my glass, trying to calm myself.

The Queen was crazy. Dangerous, violent, and utterly unhinged.

We could not let her win.

"Did she hurt you?" Mazrith asked me quietly.

"No, not really."

Frima looked at me. "She tried to get in your head?"

"Yes."

"How did you stop her?"

"I don't know. Something forced her out." I looked at Maz. "Your headband, I assume?"

He nodded slowly, but there something in his eyes that made me think there was more to it, something he wasn't saying. "Lord Dakkar has just arrived with his wife," he said instead.

I looked at the entrance, where a group of earth-fae had arrived, Dakkar at its center. "I guess I should go and ask him if they really did choose to give up this round of the *Leikmot*," I said.

CHAPTER 25
REYNA

"Lord Dakkar."

The lean earth-fae Lord was wearing a green cape shaped like one large leaf, his chest was bare, and his trousers were animal-hide, stitched together with vines.

Khadra was wearing a dress made from hundreds of green flowers, the top shaping a large fan across her chest and the skirt clinging and flowy. Her hair was braided with tiny yellow daisies.

"Ah. Little human," Dakkar said when he saw me, his easy smile spreading over his face. "Although you currently look little like a human, and a lot like a fae," he said.

Khadra gave me an appraising look. "I like it," she said. "It suits you."

I smiled awkwardly. "Thank you. You look very beautiful." Khadra gave me a confident nod and a smile of thanks. "How was your journey here?"

Both of them lost their amiable smiles immediately. "We have had better journeys," Khadra murmured darkly.

"Why? What happened?"

"We were watched."

My stomach lurched, discomfort washing over me. "Watched?"

"Eyes along the root river, all the way. In the void, beyond the bark," Dakkar said.

"Eyes? Belonging to who?" But I knew the answer. We'd seen them ourselves. *The Starved Ones.*

Dakkar tilted his head at me, his eyes narrowing. "I see in your face that you already know the answer to that question," he said.

I sighed. "We saw them too," I admitted quietly.

"This world darkens," Khadra said, then cast her eyes toward the ballroom doors. "Though this infernal Court could use some shade."

"You do not like the Gold Court?"

"Not so far, no. It is too bright, and gaudy. There is no humility here. And I do not trust a single gold-fae I have met so far."

"Why did you have the *Leikmot* moved here?" I said, leaning on the opportunity.

They looked at each other. "A messenger was sent to check on our progress with setting up the games. They were unimpressed with how far we had got and I

186

mentioned that we were... lacking in human help," Dakkar said carefully, and Khadra dropped her gaze to the ground. "Next thing we knew, we got the same message as you. That the next round would be hosted here."

That could mean it was true that the Earth Court wasn't in a fit state to host the games, but it could also have been exactly the excuse that was needed.

"Where is Lord Orm?" Khadra asked her lip curling as she said his name.

"He doesn't appear to be here," I said, but Dakkar shook his head and pointed.

Standing beside the dais with the thrones was the gold-fae Lord, wearing his usual glamorous robes and a smile on his beautiful face.

"Shame. I had hoped to be spared his company," I muttered.

"I see Lady Kaldar over there. I will bid her hello, and then we must see the Queen," Khadra said, laying her hand on Dakkar's shoulder.

I took her hint and nodded at them both. "See you tomorrow, and I hope you enjoy the ball."

"Any chance to dance with her, I shall enjoy," Dakkar said, his easy grin slipping back as he stared adoringly at his wife. She slapped his shoulder playfully, and they strode toward the ice-fae group.

I returned to Maz and Frima and told them what he had said.

"That doesn't help at all," sighed Frima. Her gaze

ELIZA RAINE

drifted to the tables of food. "I'm going to get something to eat."

When she had left us alone, I looked at Maz. "What happened with the headband? There was something you were hiding."

"I do not think it was the headband that forced her magic out. I would have felt it. Describe the feeling."

I did, and his eyes danced with interest. "My magic will never feel like water. And besides, the headband doesn't work like that. Some magic in you repelled her, Reyna."

I blinked at him. My own magic had forced her out? "So... I can protect my own head?"

He watched me finish my drink, then took my hand. "Let us go for a walk. I have an idea."

I took his hand and he led me out of two ornate stone and gild doors set in the wall opposite the harpist. Fae were moving in and out of the them, laughing and talking.

"Where are we going?"

"A garden, if I have read the fleeting thoughts of those seeking privacy correctly," he said.

I looked at him. "You just read others' minds as you're standing there?"

"No. I get impressions from people. What they want, or fear, mostly."

"That's what I get when I can see through their eyes! It's an impression of their strongest emotion at that point, not their actual thoughts."

We reached the doors and as he had said, there was a garden outside, but it wasn't like the other gardens I had seen in the Gold Court. It was more like a maze. High hedges set with twinkling lights and golden roses spread out before us, wrought iron tables and chairs for two set up in discreet corners and golden fountains carved with eagles and other birds of prey standing in the center of the larger clearings. Couples were standing in corners, embracing, or flirting, giggling as we passed.

"Here." Mazrith sat down at a table surrounded by enough plush green foliage to provide a good amount of shade, and gestured for me to sit too. "It occurs to me that this is the perfect place for you to try and use your magic. Deliberately. There are so many powerful magic users here that it would be completely disguised, and easy to blame on someone else, if anything went wrong."

Unease crawled over my skin. "You mean... I won't get anybody killed here."

"Exactly. No shadow beasts, but plenty of useful people to spy on."

"Maz, I can't control the visions, you know that."

"I know that you have never tried."

I jumped in surprise as a flurry of white caught my attention, then Voror landed on the latticework table between us.

"I agree with the fae entirely," he said.

"Hello to you too," I muttered.

Maz raised his brows. "Well? I'm going to bet that your owl agrees with me."

189

"He does," I sighed.

"I am not *your* owl," said Voror.

I relayed his words, putting my chin on my fist. "Are you really going to make me do this?"

His eyes sparked with light. "Reyna, I know you. I know you want to be able to control this power. Do not let fear win."

He was right. This was the perfect place to try. And if it worked... If it worked, then I would give myself a massive advantage in the *Leikmot*.

"Fine. What do I do?"

"I can only tell you what I do, but it's somewhere to start. Choose somebody, concentrate on their face, and allow yourself to be absorbed by their mind."

I frowned. "Allow yourself to be absorbed?"

"Yes."

"What if I can't see them?"

"Picture them. If that does not work you can try the other way. When I am in a group I do not have to concentrate on a face, I can instead search for a feeling. I concentrate on that feeling, like fear, or lust, and those emitting it will become obvious to me."

I took a deep breath, and closed my eyes. Who could I picture who's thoughts I wanted to get into? My thoughts immediately landed on Queen Andask, and my eyes flew open.

"What's wrong?"

"I thought of the Queen, but I'm as sure as Freya is honorable that I do not want to get in her head."

Alarm flitted over Mazrith's face and Voror fluttered his wings in agitation. "Stay the fuck away from Queen Andask's mind," he hissed. "Trust me. It is highly protected. You would possibly not survive an attempt."

"Understood." As I spoke, a couple walked past us, the gold-fae female leaning on the male's arm and smiling happily. She saw me and her face changed, a sneer taking her lips.

I focused as hard as I could on her face, and imagined what Maz had said, that I was being sucked into her mind, absorbed by her thoughts.

Darkness flicked over my vision, and then I was looking through her eyes, walking through the gardens, between the hedges. "I can't believe she is competing," she was whispering. Lust for the male she was hanging off was her predominant emotion. "A human thrall? What were they thinking, letting her be a champion?"

The male laughed. "With any luck, we'll get to see her fuck it all up and die while she's here."

Die? People were so disdainful of me they wished to see me die?

As indignation and anger washed through me, I saw another couple, kissing fervently under a small apple tree.

As if my magic no longer wanted to be inside the shallow female who wanted to see me die's head, darkness flicked, and I jumped heads, now in the male who was kissing.

Fierce desire enveloped my brain as he broke the kiss,

stared into the dilated eyes of a panting female, then I could see nothing as he closed his eyes and presumably continued his kiss.

Panicking that I was about to be privy to something much more personal, darkness flashed again.

"Are we all prepared for tomorrow?"

"Yes, chief. The targets are set up, and the weapon was spelled as you asked."

I was in a human guard's head, and he was talking to a gold-fae male with more braids than I could count. The only emotion I could pick up was mild stress.

"Good. As per Orm's instructions, of course?"

"Of course, chief."

The gold-fae nodded, then the guard turned and stared out over the dance floor until he saw Lord Orm, dancing with a gold-fae female in a very short white dress.

"Orm is unbeatable with a bow, but we can't risk him losing in his own Court."

I watched through the guard's eyes as Orm bowed to the female as the song finished, then strode over to Dakkar.

Wanting to hear what they were saying, I looked for somebody nearby to hop to.

An ice-fae female who was sitting down and swaying slightly, perhaps having drunk too much, looked close enough. I concentrated, and with a flash, I was in her mind.

Confusion was the dominant emotion, and I figured I

was right that she was drunk. I listened, but could only hear the hum of general chatter around me.

Praying that it worked, I willed the female to stand up. She did, unsteadily, and amazement zipped through me. But at the surge of my own emotion, the vision clouded.

Concentrate!

It sharpened again, and I willed the female to turn around just in time to see Queen Andask snatch Orm's arm and whirl him before he reached Dakkar.

"You said it would be subtle," she growled at Orm. I barely heard her words and willed the ice-fae female to crouch down, as though attending to the strap on her shoe.

"It is not as easy as that," said Orm, levelly.

"It is blatantly clear that she is not herself. You have—"

The ice-fae female squeaked as a human thrall tripped over her, spilling an entire tray of drinks.

I heard the clattering of glass, then I was gasping for breath, back inside my own head in the garden.

Mazrith and Voror were both staring at me.

I sucked in air, my hands shaking in excitement. "Oh, fates," I breathed. "Oh, Freya and fates. It worked."

CHAPTER 26

REYNA

I was tripping over my words as I told Mazrith and Voror what had just happened. I didn't know if I was more excited about what I had been able to do, hopping between heads and willing movement, or what I had actually learned from doing it.

"The Prince was right, this is an excellent place to practice spying," said Voror. "My hearing is good, but in indoor crowds such as this one I would never be able to make out individual conversations."

"I think you should try to enter Dakkar's mind," Mazrith said thoughtfully.

"No!" My reaction was instinctive. "Absolutely not."

"I wish to know if we can trust him."

"I'd be better off getting into the mind of everyone in our own camp if we wanted to find out who we can trust," I snorted.

"They can all guard their minds, you would not be able to get in."

"I know. But I'm not getting in Dakkar's either. Besides, all I get is an emotion. That wouldn't tell me if I could trust him, it's not like I can see his thoughts."

"You sensed Rangvald's guilt. That was enough."

I stared at Maz, cogs turning in my head. "Wait, why wasn't *his* mind guarded?"

"It should have been," Mazrith said slowly. "I wonder if you can get past mind guards?"

"Well, I'm not about to try."

"You could try on me."

"What?"

"Try and get into my head."

"No!"

Voror fluttered his wings. "You are growing loud. Perhaps you should save this conversation for some-where more private."

I took a breath and repeated his words to Mazrith.

"The owl is wise," Maz said.

Voror clicked his beak smugly.

"I need a drink anyway," I said, standing up. Mazrith's eyes drifted over my torso as the folds of my dress tumbled over my leg.

"Yes. And Frima will be wondering on our whereabouts."

. . .

195

When we re-entered the ballroom, it was clear Frima wasn't the slightest bit concerned about our where-abouts. She was in an animated conversation with Henrik.

We moved to join her, and Khadra fixed her gaze on me as soon as we got close. "You do not have a drink."

"Oh, no I—"

"Come," she said, and strode toward a long table covered in glasses.

"Everything alright?" I asked, hurrying to keep up with her.

She turned to me, her eyes serious. "Dak is male, and therefore unable to ask for help."

"Help?"

She bit her lip, looked over my shoulder, then dropped her voice low. "Tomorrow's game is a target competition of some sort. One of our group overheard as such."

I blinked. "Why are you helping me?"

"Because if Dak doesn't win, you are the only other one I wish to see champion."

"You wouldn't prefer Lady Kaldar over a human?"

Khadra gave me a look. "I do not believe you are any normal human. A male like Prince Mazrith Andask does not bind himself, or look so flame-eyed, at any simple human."

I bristled, even though she might be right about me not being a normal human. "A human is as much enti-tled to love, or protection, or strength, or power, as a fae is." I snapped the words before I remembered that I was talking to a fae Lord's wife.

But she was looking at me as an equal. With an annoyed sigh, she set a hand on her hip. "Listen to me. I know there are rumors about how us earth-fae treat our humans. But they are not what they seem. In fact, it is because of you humans that I need Dak to win this accursed festival and gain the King's attention."

I held my hand up, shaking my head in confusion. "Woah, you've lost me. You're going to have to start at the beginning."

"No." Her bright eyes held mine. "I will not tell you anything you might use against me until I know I can trust you. Dak will not ask you, but I am, right now. If, during the games, it looks like you can not win, will you try to help Dak instead?"

I stared at her. "Presumably, you're offering for him to do the same in return?"

"Yes."

My mind raced over the proposition, landing easily on an answer. "Yes. And, I overhead something too. The game is stacked in Orm's favor somehow."

Fury whirled over her face. "Greedy, selfish, pigs-blood-quaffing gold-fae," she snarled. "Thank you for telling me."

I shrugged. "Anyone but Orm."

She nodded, her eyes hardening. "Anyone but Orm."

. . .

I told Mazrith and Frima about the conversation with Khadra as soon as I got back with my drink. Maz looked worried, but Frima agreed that it was a good idea, before returning to flirting with Henrik.

"There's no risk," I said to Maz. "Why wouldn't I agree?"

He looked around the room warily. "On the face of it, it seems sound."

"So, why are you so worried?"

"Everything about this place worries me," he answered. "We are on the precipice, *ástin mín*. I believe that what you overheard my stepmother saying to Orm was about the Gold Court Queen. They are working in tandem against her, and I suspect they have drugged or spelled her, to control her. If they believe they will be accused of such treason, they may be forced to act. We must be on our fullest alert."

"We are," I said, squeezing his arm. "And, if you're right and this might all blow up at any minute, maybe we should try to enjoy ourselves now. You did, after all, make me buy a dress." I picked up the skirt and swooshed it, smiling.

He stepped into me, gripping my waist with his large hands and making my breath catch. "Do you remember the first ball we attended together?" I nodded. "Every male there wanted you. Wanted a taste of you."

Heat swirled through my body as his eyes darkened.

"Well, you've had a taste," I whispered. "What did you think?"

"You are too divine for them to even consider," he growled. "But that does not stop them. They are all imagining you now, lusting after you." His chest rumbled. "Once more, they need to be shown what is mine."

Before I could say a word, his arm was wrapped around my waist, and I was being spun toward the dance floor.

Couples parted, allowing us to swirl into the center of the area, eyes fixed on us.

Mazrith, huge, dark and hulking, his black furs, hair and silver circlet catching the light, and me, a whirl of black and gold, topped with copper.

"Well, they're looking now," I whispered as Mazrith tipped me back, in time with the lively music.

"As they should, when you are wrapped around me," he rumbled.

The music changed to something slower, far more sensual, and Mazrith straightened, pulling me against him.

"The runes," I said, as one drifted from his cheek.

His eyes narrowed, then he rolled me down his arm, so that my body was no longer pressed to his, but our fingers were still intertwined. He lifted his arm high, turning me beneath it. His other hand moved to the staff at his hip, and then he twirled me back into him.

"Maz, you mustn't—" I started, then gasped. The cool whisper of his shadows fluttered against my ankles, then flowed up the inside of my leg.

He turned me again, so that I was further from him, but still clutching his hand.

My eyes swept over him and his staff, but the trickle of shadow was so fine nobody would know it was there.

Except me. There was no way I wouldn't notice — the shadows had reached my inner thigh, and I locked my eyes on his.

"Maz...." I said on a breath, the shadows swirling around both thighs now, teasing and tingling.

Shadows swirled in his irises as he turned me again, moving expertly to the music. Couples moved in similar dances all around us, most pressed tighter together than we were, but all casting frequent glances at us.

"Yes, *ástin mín?*" The shadows kissed higher, sweeping over me, hidden under my huge skirts.

I gasped, and almost stumbled. Mazrith moved, his hand still holding mine, the dance continuing. "Do you see any runes?" He asked so quietly only I could hear him.

I shook my head. His sultry, predatory smile took his face, and I forced myself not to step into him, wrap my legs around his massive thighs, take his mouth with mine.

The shadows flowed over me again, this time moving beneath the silk of my underwear.

I clamped my lips tightly together to stop a moan escaping, and Mazrith's eyes flared with unbridled lust. The beat of the music deepened, the tone speeding, and the shadows moved with it, flicking over me, finding my clit.

I clenched Mazrith's hand tight as he twirled me, my eyes skimming those of the other couples as the shadows flicked, kissing, teasing, making me ache.

My every nerve was alight, adrenaline coursing through me, as strong and heady as my desire.

"More?" This time his voice was in my head, and unable to answer, I nodded.

More. Always more. Never stop.

The teasing flicks over my clit continued, but a whisper of cool, then a gentle pressure found my wet entrance.

This time, a moan did escape me, and Maz's control flickered. His expression was so heated for a moment I feared he might abandon the hidden shadows and take me right there.

But the control returned, and the pressure increased. Slowly, in time with the beat, his shadows pressed into my aching heat. My knees weakened, Maz's grip on my hand tightening as he moved me over the dance floor, my feet unsteady.

I bumped into a woman in huge white feathers, and she sneered at me. But I barely registered her face.

The flicking over my clit quickened, the pressure increasing, as the shadows moved deeper inside me, swirling, stretching, pulsing.

The pressure inside me was growing, becoming uncontainable, and the room around me became a blur.

"Maz," I gasped, and he twirled me into him, supporting my weight as my legs buckled, my orgasm ripping through me.

"Come for me, my Queen, *ástin mín,*" he said inside my head, and waves of pleasure rolled from my core, ricocheting through my entire body as he turned me on the dance floor, the other couples moving around us.

He rolled me back out to arm's length, still gripping my hand, and I stumbled, blinking, trying to keep my hands from shaking as the shadows flowed around me, stroking gently, keeping shudders of pleasure rocking through me.

I tried not to look at the others, tried not to see if they had noticed. Mazrith's smile returned as he moved me over the dance floor. I was trying to keep from panting, desperately trying to compose myself, and his voice spoke in my mind again, his eyes ablaze when I focused on them. "You are mine. And I do not care who sees."

CHAPTER 27

REYNA

"I still can't believe you did that," I whispered, as we reached the entrance to Mazrith's tent.

"They needed to know you belong to me. That you have everything you need, *from me.*" His words were a growl, and he had been tight and husky since we left.

I may have found my release, but he had taken none. Tingles of shocked pleasure rippled through me, caused by both embarrassment and the utter, delighted disbelief that he could do that to me, *like that*. In secret, in front of hundreds of other folk.

Taking a breath, I forced my mind back to what else had happened at the ball.

I lifted the flap of Mazrith's tent, and he made that deep rumbling in his chest that I loved and slightly feared.

"If you enter this tent, I will not be responsible for my

actions." Heat thrilled through me, but again, I forced my desire down.

"Maz, I want you to do something for me."

"Anything. Especially if you have this dress on when I do it." His eyes roved over my body, and I thumped his arm.

"Maz, concentrate! This is important."

He stared at me a moment, visibly controlling himself, the bright light making his eyes narrow.

"What do you want me to do?" he asked eventually, his voice calmer, but still strained.

"You made me try something tonight, and it worked."

"Succumbing to my shadow magic in front of—"

I held my hand out, covering his lips and silencing him.

"Magic, Maz." I glanced around, ensuring we were alone. "I want you to try again with the staff."

I expected him to argue with me, but instead he opened the flap of his tent wide and gestured me inside. The firepit in the middle was just embers and the tent canvas was thick enough that there was finally some respite from the incessant brightness.

I pulled the staff from where I had secretly secured it around my thigh. His eyes darkened at the exposure of my leg, and he dragged his attention back to the staff when I passed it to him.

"What makes you think this will be any different than before?"

I shrugged. "Last time you tried, I couldn't run around through folk's heads. Everything is changing, all the time. What have we got to lose?"

He gazed at me a minute, then took a step back and closed his eyes. Reminded that last time I'd watched him do this he was completely naked, I found myself looking at trousers, then blushing.

I was silent as he held the staff, long moments passing by. Eventually, he opened his eyes. "I'm sorry, *ástin mín*. It still does not accept me."

He handed it back to me, and I sighed as I peered at the lifeless wood. "I had hoped to be sent a memory vision that would tell us what to do by now."

"*You* could try and connect with it."

"What?" I gaped at him.

"Your ears were not pointed before. Your magic is developing, as you just pointed out."

"No, I…" I looked between him and the staff, and my protestations died on my lips. He was right. Hadn't I just told him that everything was changing, all the time? "What do you have to do?"

"Just will yourself into the wood. You'll know if it works."

Could I really make a staff work? *A mist-staff*?

Was that what we were missing?

Buoyed by the completely unexpected response of my attempt at magic earlier, I gripped the staff tight, and squeezed my eyes shut. With every ounce of concentration I could muster, I willed myself to connect with the wood.

Nothing happened.

"It was worth a try," Maz said, when I finally opened my eyes and gave him a sad smile. A slight headache washed through my skull as I forced my arms to relax.

"Everything is worth a try," I muttered.

He stepped toward me, cupping my cheek. "Your tenacity is one of your most beautiful features. You know that?"

"I do now," I smiled at him.

My tenacity had been a weapon, usually the thing that made others so angry with me. Now, somebody loved me for it. And it made me feel like I was ten feet taller. A hundred beasts braver.

"I don't want anyone to take this away from us, Maz," I whispered, emotion overwhelming my voice. "We just found each other."

"I'm going nowhere. Whatever happens." But I could see the tightness in his eyes, across his jaw.

We would die if the Queen won. In fact, our fate would likely be worse than death.

I stood up on my tiptoes to kiss him, and a golden rune floated from his lips before I got there.

I cursed as he stepped backward, anger flashing first over his features, then hard resolve. The fiery passion had doused, sudden charged emotion replacing it. "I'm am sorry, *ástin mín*, but I will need all the power I can get in the coming days, I am sure. Much as I want to kiss you, I would sooner save your life if required."

I smiled at him. "I mean, they're mighty fine kisses, but yeah. You're probably right. Maz, if anything happens during the games tomorrow that looks like it might kill me, fuck the rules of the festival — come and save me." I smiled at him. "We'll start the fight ourselves."

"Fight, fuck, repeat," he said drily, then smiled back. "It is not a terrible way of life."

I laughed, but two more runes floated from his skin. We both watched them, falling silent, until Maz spoke. "I fear I only have days of magic left now," he said softly.

"Then, I shall bid you goodnight. Maz, I love you."

"I love you too, Reyna."

I couldn't sleep, though, once I was in my comfortable bed beside Frima's.

I knew we couldn't risk losing his magic just to be intimate, but that didn't stop me fantasizing about him, and of every single intimate thing I knew he could do to me when this was over. To stop myself from raiding the camp to find some fae-wine to induce the dreams I so desperately wanted, I grabbed Tait's book from my pack instead.

If I couldn't sleep and I couldn't be with Mazrith,

maybe I could find out something useful. We were, after all, running out of time.

I flicked through looking for the word mist and stopped when I found it.

There was a long and flowing description by the author of the primordial mists that the whole of *Yggdrasil* was formed from, followed by a description of the origin of staffs as conduits for magic.

"The High-Fae, also known as Vanir, were originally created by Freya, and endowed with powerful psychic magic. When the five elemental fae were created, the Vanir were charged with keeping watch over them. In order to balance their power with those others who resided in Yggdrasil, it was decided that they must use staffs to wield power, and they would not be able to create the staffs themselves. The Vanir created ten mist-staffs, as examples for what would become known as the rune-marked.

These staffs were incredibly powerful and had long memories, tied to their wielders. It is not known at this time where the staffs are, or if they have survived, since the Vanir left our world with the gods they serve."

I kept reading, the passages confirming what Tait had already told me about how the staffs were originally distributed. There was nothing about how to make them accept a new wielder, or them rejecting wielders.

With a sigh, I thumbed through the pages of the old book. Something on a page caught my eye, and I stopped.

Runes, *moving.*

The actual script was moving on the page, flickering in and out of focus.

I sat up, squinting, convinced I must have dozed off and was half asleep.

But, I hadn't. The words were flickering on the pages, dancing around so that I couldn't understand them.

Only five marks were still, and I recognized them all. The marks of the rune-marked.

I lifted the book, desperately trying to catch words as they danced and blurred on the page.

"...*Choose their rune*..."

"...*magic of the Vanir*..."

I frowned, trying to concentrate, frustration building. Then two words flashed into focus, and my mouth fell open.

"...*copper hair*..."

CHAPTER 28

REYNA

I scrambled out of bed, clutching the book. Making my way out of my tent I skipped across the camp to Tait's, slipping inside.

"Tait?" I hissed.

There were two beds, and Ellisar sat bolt-upright in one of them, swiping up an axe and facing me. His face relaxed as I threw my hands up.

"It's me! I need to talk to Tait. Urgently."

The shadow-spinner rolled over and sat up slowly, blinking before reaching for his spectacles. "Reyna?"

"Yes. Tait, I need to use your truth glass thing. Please," I added, then looked at Ellisar. "And I'm sorry, but would you mind leaving a moment?"

Ellisar gave me a look but flung back the covers and climbed out of bed.

I whirled, stifling a gasp at the fact that he was

completely naked. A moment later he lumbered past me, trousers pulled up but still untied.

"Thanks," I said, trying not to blush. "One more thing. Do you think you could grab Maz for me?"

"Anything for our future Queen," he said, with a mock bow, then left the tent.

I hurried over to Tait and sat down on the edge of his mattress. "Tait, look."

He peered at the page, then looked at me with vague concern. "It's the five marks of the rune-marked," he said.

"Yes, but look at the other runes. Are they all moving around and coming in and out of focus?"

His look of vague concern deepened to full concern. "There are no other runes on the page. Are you feeling well? Did you drink much at the ball?" He reached out a hand and pressed it to my forehead.

Mazrith appeared at the tent flap, and Voror entered with him. Maz frowned when he saw me. "You are in another male's tent, wearing naught but a shift," he rumbled.

I rolled my eyes, and batted Tait's hand away. "Look." I held up the book. "This is a very old book Tait has about staff-making. There is a page in here with runes that I can't focus on, but I caught a few of them. One of them said copper-hair."

Both males looked at me a beat, then Tait began to rummage in a pile of things by his bed. Mazrith moved closer as he handed me the truth glass.

Anticipation making my pulse quicken, I held it over the page of runes. Instantly, they settled, coming into sharp focus.

I took a breath, then read aloud.

"The rune-marked are a powerful subset of the high-fae, charged with great magic that allows them to craft staff for the other fae of Yggdrasil. Endowed with some of the psychic magic of the Vanir, they are able to get impressions of people, so as to ensure their staffs are a perfect match. They may change the mark on the wrist to any listed here and choose the rune they wish to work with that day, making them *gold-givers, shadow-spinners, water-winders, fire-forgers and wood-workers*." I stared at Maz and Tait.

"Rune-marked could *choose* which magic to work with?" Tait breathed.

I continued reading. "The rune-marked fae always appeared with copper hair and were revered by humans and fae alike. Like the Vanir, they did not need staffs themselves to conduct magic, instead relying on spirit animals."

I dropped the book into my lap, my mouth hanging open as I looked at Voror.

"Spirit animal?" I breathed.

The owl blinked back at me. "This is not something I am familiar with," he said.

"Keep reading," said Mazrith softly.

I picked the book back up. There was only one more

line. "Long may the rune-marked wield their power well and keep the balance of magic true in *Yggdrasil*."

"This makes no sense," muttered Mazrith. "Clearly the rune-marked do not have the powers described on that page."

"It makes perfect sense," I whispered. "Tait, I saw your shadow runes, when I watched you spin." Tait's mouth fell open. "I can use mind magic," I said, pointing a shaking finger at the line about getting impressions of people. "Without a staff, but only with an animal nearby." I moved my shaking finger to Voror.

"This book calls them the rune-marked fae?" Mazrith crouched in front of me.

"Yes," I nodded.

"But, the rune-marked of our world are human." Tait and I both nodded. "So, something changed between this being written and now."

"And there was an attempt to hide it. Only Reyna, who is apparently not a human rune-marked, but a fae rune-marked, could see the script," Tait breathed.

"So, I am a fae?" I whispered.

"Yes. But, a rune-marked fae. Not gold or shadow fae. Rune-marked. Something you have aways been."

I dragged comfort, and stability, from his words, trying to slow my racing thoughts. I had always been rune-marked. Always something apart from most humans, able to see and connect to magic.

The fear of being a fae wasn't bubbling up inside me, wasn't threatening to overwhelm me.

I wasn't one of them. I was something else. The full version of what I had always been, perhaps?

Mazrith was smiling gently at me, and I longed to reach for his hand, but stopped myself.

"What changed? Why did the rune-marked become human, and why am I changing into a fae since you took me?"

"I don't know, *ástin min*," he said. "But this is more than we knew before. Your magic comes from the high-fae, you do not need a staff to use it, but you do need Voror nearby. And, you may be able to craft staffs from all of the elements."

"Not just gold?" The realization made a smile come to my lips. The fascination I had always had with the staffs of the other fae had pervaded my whole life. Now I knew why.

Like pieces of a puzzle finally slotting into place, some restless part of me that never fully settled was quieting, a sense of reassurance replacing it.

I still had a hundred questions, and no idea where I came from, but for the first time in my life I knew why I was different.

We spent another hour talking, but we got no more information or clarification from the script, just ideas and theories.

Tait believed the rune-marked became human when the Vanir left with the gods.

Mazrith guessed that there were both human and fae rune-marked, and I was the last of my kind, or the first in a new line.

I didn't know what I believed, except that I was something else. Something that didn't exist in *Yggdrasil* anywhere else.

Somebody had sent Voror to me, though. Somebody was guiding the visions. That had to be a Vanir, didn't it? The script had said that the rune-marked were a type of Vanir, created by them, and shared their magic.

"What do you think, Voror?" I whispered to the owl, once we were back in my tent, Frima gently snoring in the other bed.

Mazrith had insisted I get some sleep before the game the next day, but we both knew that was unlikely.

"The fae who sent me to you had hair made of light," Voror said. "Is this a trait of the Vanir?"

"I don't know, but it sounds feasible to me," I said.

"Then we are in agreement. The Vanir have awakened your fae rune-marked magic."

"But why?" And perhaps more alarmingly, what did any of this have to do with the Starved Ones? Had the Vanir also been responsible for my visions of the monsters?

"I believe we will find out in due course. In the meantime, Queen Andask poses a threat to your life and Mazrith's, and you need to concentrate on that."

"Easier said than done," I muttered. "You haven't just found out you're from an extinct race."

"Rune-marked are not extinct, nor are fae. And you already knew you were both."

I glared up at him where he perched by the hole in the top of the tent. "So you're saying there's no big revelation here?"

"No, it is useful to know. But it changes nothing. You need to survive the *Leikmot*, and it is nearly dawn."

"Fine. But I'm not going to be able to sleep."

In fact, I did sleep. The overwhelm of the day caught up with me mere moments after Voror left the tent. My last thought before I succumbed to sleep was that the owl was right. Nothing had changed — I still needed to try to win the games.

But now I was a fae competing, with magic I knew how to use.

CHAPTER 29
REYNA

The next morning Frima woke me up by throwing a pillow at me. "Rise and shine. Time to train."

I rolled over, grabbing the pillow and shoving it under my head. "Breakfast," I mumbled.

"You know, for an ex-slave you have a lot of demands."

I scrabbled to a sitting position and launched the pillow back at her. She caught it, laughing. I blinked around the tent, everything that happened the day before flooding back.

I was a rune-marked fae, and I had used my magic to skip through other's heads like it was natural.

Swallowing, I steeled myself.

There was no time for overwhelm, or constant questions on loop in my head.

Voror was right — there was no way right now to

217

find out more, so I should concentrate on the games. Nothing had truly changed, except that my fear of this new magic was lessening.

"How did it go with Henrik?" I asked Frima casually, clambering out of the warm, comfortable bed and making my way to one of the side areas that was filled with clothes. I rooted around for sturdy trousers and my feather-styled chain-mail armor, attempting to keep my thoughts level.

"Good. You know, there's more to him than I thought there was."

"Oh yeah?" I looked at her over my shoulder. "More than just sex, you mean?"

"I didn't have sex with him," she sighed, before brightening. "But look, he stole this for me." She threw something small at me, and I instinctively reached out to catch it. "Takes some guts to steal gold from a gold-fae."

Her words reached me too late. My fingers had already closed around the small gold dolphin.

"Frima!"

"What?"

"I'm a *gold-giver*, you can't just throw gold at me!"

"Why not?"

I dropped the tiny golden statue, scooping up my clothes. "Because!"

"Why are you being so weird? Reyna why— Reyna!"

I crashed to the floor as the first wave hit me.

Shadows. Mildew and rot. The sense that something was horribly wrong.

It lifted and I felt around the fur-covered ground, trying to steady myself. Frima was crouched beside me. "Reyna, I'm sorry. What did I do?"

"Nothing, it'll pass," I mumbled quickly, and the second wave came.

The screeching laugh, flashes of red in the dark, figures moving, indistinct. The sense of wrongness shifted to fear.

The vision lifted.

"Do I need to get Maz?"

The third wave came before I could answer her.

The splitting scream, and the smell of blood.

But the laugh didn't follow the scream, and the figures weren't indistinct. It was her. The Elder.

The vision lifted and I gasped for breath, fear making me sweat and tremble.

I knew the fourth vision was coming.

And it did.

She was there, inches from me, her face mutilated and raw, her missing skin and bones slimy and putrid. "We saw you on the river. We know where you are. It will not be long now."

The vision lifted, the cloying smell of death making me swipe at my face and gasp for the warm, smoky air in the tent.

"Reyna?" Frima sounded panicked, and I turned slowly to her, blinking hard, trying to focus. "Shit, you're pale. What do you need? What is happening? Are you pregnant?"

Her words jolted me back to reality. "Pregnant?" I shook my head thickly. "I'm not pregnant."

"Then what in the name of Freya just happened?"

I stared up into her worried face, then let out a long, shaky breath. It seemed one more person was about to know my secrets.

Frima sat quietly while I told her everything. She didn't look surprised or confused at any point, and when she asked questions, they were clipped and to the point.

"So, that's how you've been helping Maz find the mist-staff? With visions?"

"Yes."

"What did you just see, then?"

I swallowed hard. "The Starved Ones. The Elder who sang at me in the woods, that Arthur tore to bits."

She stared at me as Mazrith burst into the tent, Voror swooping in behind him.

"Are you alright?"

"I'm fine. How did you—"

"Voror." Maz crouched down in front of me, peering into my face with concern. "What happened?"

"I touched some gold Frima has, and it triggered a vision, that's all," I reassured him.

"What did you see?"

"The Elder. She said she knows where I am."

Something that may have been fear crossed

Mazrith's hard face. He glanced at Frima, then back at me. "Reyna, my power is waning."

"And you're the only one strong enough to stop an Elder," said Frima gravely.

"Yes. I certainly can't stop both the Queen *and* the Starved Ones. If they attack..."

"They wouldn't attack the Gold Court palace, surely? They've never ventured into the heart of the Courts," she said.

Maz shook his head. "The attacks on our periphery were getting bolder. Before.... Before I found you." He turned back to me. "Did you learn anything that might help us?"

I shook my head. "Nothing."

He sighed. "Frima, keep that gold with you," he said.

She nodded, scooping up the little dolphin. "I'm sorry, Reyna. I didn't know."

"I know. It's fine. Please, keep what I've told you to yourself," I said awkwardly.

She snorted. "I understand why you would keep that a secret, Reyna. As if I'd be marching around telling people that I have visions of monsters." She shook her head. "You know, I'm starting to understand why you're so..." She cast around. "You," she finished.

I cocked my head. "Is that a compliment?"

"Yes. I guess. Look, there are hours until the game and you need to get your head straight. Plus, a target game could be bows, but it could also be axes and you haven't had any axe-throwing practice. Are you still up for training?"

"Absolutely."

Maz offered to help me with my armor, but I was nervous that any contact between us would further accelerate the loss of his mom's magic, so I asked Frima to help instead. Promising to wait outside with coffee and pastry, he left the tent.

"Come, there are axes we can practice with in Svangrior's tent. He's practically turned the place into an armory," muttered Frima when we were both ready.

Svangrior and Ellisar's tent was indeed more of an armory than a bedroom. Everything was stacked in piles around two low, hay-stuffed mattresses where the males slept.

Frima began to rummage through piles of metal spears. "It wouldn't hurt to try spear throwing too," she mused, inspecting some of the javelins.

I moved to another pile of sacks, looking for axes, and froze as I moved two large bags of chain mail.

"That's..." I reached out, lifting the small black canvas bag in front of me up. "That's *my* bag."

Frima came over to me, frowning. "Your bag?"

I opened it, careful not to touch the contents. There, nestled in an old shirt, was the gold staff-top Lhoris had given to me.

I let out a long breath. "I stole some gold when I fled

the Gold Court, and I ended up bringing it here. I thought I might use it to buy my way out."

"What happened to it?"

"It was stolen."

"Stolen?"

"Yes. From my rooms during the first few days I was in the Shadow Court." Frima's eyes widened as I continued. "Around the same time as the snake was put in my bedroom."

"No. That means... Svangrior?"

"Or Ellisar. This is his room too, right?"

Frima shook her head disbelievingly. "Ellisar has no magic. He couldn't have gotten into your room."

I swallowed. "Where is Svangrior?"

"I'm not sure. Let me get Maz."

She returned a moment later with the Prince, and I showed him the bag. His face clouded with anger. "It may be time to enter my warrior's mind after all."

CHAPTER 30

REYNA

But Svangrior was nowhere to be seen when we left the tent.

"I saw him an hour ago," said Tait, who was sitting by the main campfire with his gauze eye-guard, an open book and the truth glass on his lap. "But not since."

"He took some pie and left the camp, my Lady," said Brynja, handing out mugs of nettle tea and coffee.

Tait nodded. "That he did."

Mazrith scowled out toward the huge, glittering palace. "Everyone, be on your guard."

Ellisar stood from where he and Kara had been playing chess. "Why? Is he in trouble?"

"I don't know. Just tell me if you see him."

The big human nodded. "Sure thing. I see an earth-fae." He pointed and we all looked.

Dakkar and Henrik were making their way toward our camp.

"Lord Dakkar," I said, moving to greet him before Maz could get to him.

"Reyna," he said.

"That is the first time you've called me by name."

He gave me a rueful smile. "Apparently, my wife has decided that we are friends."

I smiled back as Frima and Maz came to stand either side of me. "Then do I call you by your first name?"

He laughed. "Not unless you are my mother. Dak. My friends call me Dak." His easy expression turned serious. "Look. I did not ask my wife to speak with you last night or make the offer she did. But I do share her feelings about you." He looked at Maz. "About both of you. For what it is worth, I would much rather see you on the throne before your stepmother."

"As would I," muttered Maz.

Dakkar looked back at me. "Khadra told me that you said the game was rigged in Orm's favor." Henrik's face tightened in annoyance next to him.

"Yes. I overheard a guard."

He nodded his head in thanks. "I appreciate you passing that on."

"As I said to your wife, I would rather anyone than Orm won this thing."

"Agreed. As such, I wish to talk to you about her suggestion."

"That if it looks like you can't win, you'll do what you can to help me, and I'll do the same in return?"

His smile returned, cocky this time. "But understand, little human, that I *will* win. And I will not sabotage my own chances to help you."

I gave him a dry smile. "That makes two of us."

Dakkar held out his hand. "Then it is agreed. Good luck, Reyna."

I shook his hand. "And to you, Dak."

We all watched the two earth-fae left, and Frima grunted. "I want to trust him."

"Me too."

Mazrith looked sideways at me. "Did you enter his head?"

I gave him a look. "You know I didn't."

He surprised me by shrugging. "Trust your instinct Reyna. And know that I will kill anyone before they get a chance to hurt you."

I beamed at him, and Frima rolled her eyes.

"Ellisar, grab me a bag of axes would you?" she called, then punched me on the shoulder. "Eat up, then we train."

"Train?" asked Kara, from just behind us. We turned to her. "Can I join in?"

I looked to Frima, who grinned. "I swear on Freya, I will never say no to that. The more females who can defend themselves, the better."

. . .

We had been hurling axes at Frima's shadowy targets for almost an hour when Mazrith stood.

"It is time. Are you ready?"

I dropped the axe I was holding into its sack and scooped up my bow. "As I'll ever be."

"You sure as Freya look ready," said Kara, her face flushed from throwing axes.

Mazrith's eyes were fixed on me behind his gauze protection, filled with what I was sure was pride. I felt a surge of desire to see what I looked like through his eyes, but I tamped it down, beaming at him instead.

In all my chainmail, with staffs and bows and arrows strapped to my body, my finger talons secured and the braid in my hair, I guessed I really did look different to the slave that had arrived in the Shadow Court.

I didn't just look different. I *was* different.

All the fears I'd had, the anger, the need to run... Everything had changed.

But mostly? I was no longer alone.

I'd always had my friends but I knew my life wouldn't end in the palace workshop. I'd always known I didn't belong there. Now I knew exactly where I belonged, and it wasn't a place at all. It was with the Prince of the Shadow Court.

He stared into my eyes, mirroring my every feeling.

Lhoris stood up from his seat at the fire, moving next to Mazrith and casting his eyes over me. "The armor is a little too fae for my tastes, but strength and power suits you, Reyna."

"Thank you, Lhoris."

He moved to give me a stoic hug, and I kissed him on the cheek. "Earn another braid, Reyna," he said.

"I'll do my best."

He released me, and I turned. "Kara—" She barreled straight into me, hugging me hard around my armor. "Stay here, and stay safe. If Svangrior comes, stay with Ellisar," I whispered to her.

"*You* stay safe. And good luck. Kick them all in the baby-makers."

I laughed. Ellisar's language was rubbing off on her. "Good plan."

"Good luck, Reyna. Do everything I would, and nothing I wouldn't," said Frima, hand on her hip.

I let go of Kara and looked at the fierce female warrior. "You're not coming?"

She shook her head. "Can't leave the rune-marked without a fae when we're not sure where Svangrior is."

Relief flooded me, along with a bite of disappointment. I wanted her there. But I grabbed for her hand in thanks. "See you soon."

"May Thor lend you strength, Reyna."

CHAPTER 31

REYNA

azrith and I drew glances, as it seemed we always did, when we joined the throng of folk heading up the grand stairs to where guards were directing everyone.

We reached a flat platform that I was fairly sure was a landscaped courtyard the night before, with a small fountain decorated with a sea serpent.

The area looked completely different now though.

The fountain had been replaced with a huge pool. A statue of Skadi, goddess of archery and hunting, was in the middle of the pool, and four tiny, one-man canoes floated on the water.

Crowds of spectators were seated around it, the Queen of the Gold Court on a raised dais.

"Welcome," she said when the last few people appeared to have arrived, her voice magically amplified. "The game is simple. The first contestant to hit all of the targets positioned around the fountain will win. You may hit them with magic, weapons, whatever you wish, but all must be the same."

"That's it?" I whispered to Maz.

"I doubt it as easy as she has just implied," he said, gripping my hand. "Stay safe, Reyna. And if you can, win." He handed me my bow, and I nodded.

"I will."

Maz moved to sit with the other spectators, far from Queen Andask, and I went to where Dakkar and Orm were already standing next to the canoes in the fountain. Kaldar was approaching, and I took a second to stare up at the Skadi statue. She was twenty feet tall, her hair tied back in one thick braid, her bow drawn, and an arrow nocked. Frima had told me all about her and the great Ullr being the deities behind hunting, winter and the mountains.

May my aim be true, I sent her a small prayer, and checked the quiver at my back. It was full. I was ready.

"Board your boats!" called the Queen, when Kaldar had reached us. The crowd cheered as we all dragged the little canoes to the side and climbed in. I kept as far from Orm as I could, but I could feel his eyes on me. Kaldar was giving everybody wary glances, determination in her eyes, and Dakkar had his usual easy grin.

"Three, two, one, start!" the Queen called.

Orm instantly fired a ball of light at the target nearest us, while Dak launched a vine at it. I grabbed an oar and pushed it through the water, deciding quickly to go in the opposite direction to them, rather than get in their way.

Kaldar nocked an arrow in her bow, taking careful aim, but her canoe drifted as I passed her, my current making her rock. She threw me a glare, re-aimed, and her arrow flew straight and true, striking the target with a solid thunk.

"Time to go, Reyna," I muttered to myself.

I sped around the fountain, only wedging the oar between my legs when I couldn't see any of the other competitors anymore. I grabbed my bow, letting the momentum of my canoe carry me gently on. I nocked my arrow, drew back, and fired.

The arrow hit the target dead on, and I swiveled, sighting the next one. I waited a few seconds for the canoe to move me closer, then loosed. Another dead hit.

I kept moving, my momentum slowing, but still solid, and nocked my next arrow. Just as I released, Dakkar came into view ahead of me. I fired my arrow at the same time he did, and I barely stopped myself giving him a friendly nod.

He was my competitor, and I didn't want anyone else to know we had any kind of alliance. He didn't even make eye contact with me as he sped past, using his vines to launch little wooden darts into the targets as he went.

My momentum had slowed, so I set my bow down, swapping it for my oar, and built up some speed again. When I next picked up the bow, the fourth target in sight, Kaldar came speeding toward me. I went to steady myself, seeing that her powerful current would rock me, and paused.

She was moving so fast because the back of her boat was on fire.

Orm appeared behind her, launching balls of light not at the targets, but at her canoe. They weren't exploding though, just hovering over the back of her boat, flames flickering beneath them.

"What are you doing?" Kaldar yelled at Orm, her face a mask of fury.

If he was trying to get back at her for the game she had nearly drowned him in, then he was wasting his time — I highly doubted the fountain was deep enough to drown in.

There was a loud cracking sound, and I wasn't the only one who looked up in surprise.

The statue of Skadi was moving, and so was her bow. She was taking aim.

At Orm's balls of light.

"Kaldar!"

Orm had done it deliberately. Somehow, his lights were able to draw the fire of the statue.

I yelled again, "Kaldar, watch the statue!"

But the ice-fae ignored me, powering her boat on.

I had just sailed past my next target, I realized and forced myself to concentrate. I lifted my bow, nocked and aimed. I hit the edge of the target, but it was still a hit. I spun around, just in time to see Skadi loose a burning white ball at Kaldar's boat.

She dove out of the vessel as it hit, flames roaring from the wood.

I hissed a curse, then grabbed my oar, powering myself through the water and away from Orm. If he was as-good-as able to control the statue, then the rest of us stood no chance.

I dropped the oar on my lap, firing at two more targets, then realized I had lost count of how many were left. There must be at least four, given that I had gone around about half of the circular pool.

Glancing behind me for Orm, I considered trying to jump into his head, to see what he had planned next. But, concentrating on hitting all of the targets seemed like a better plan.

"Ignore Orm, hit the targets," said Voror into my mind, confirming my strategy.

I moved through the water, then heard a curse. Dakkar's canoe floated into view behind me, moving fast. His boat had three balls of light above it, and the Skadi statue was rotating, trying to line up its bow with the speeding vessel.

This time, Dakkar did make eye contact with me as he passed, moving three times as fast as I was.

"Hit all the targets and win," he called, quietly enough that I was sure only I heard him. "I'll draw the fire. Orm only has three left, he missed one back there."

Determined, I drew my bow, and landed two more targets, as Skadi released her arrow.

It missed Dakkar by inches, but the water rocked violently. I gripped the side of the boat and willed the current to push me through the water.

I paddled as hard as I could trying to reach the last two targets before Orm or Skadi came after me. I could hear Orm, laughing. The Skadi statute began to rotate, and I looked up to see Dakkar had changed direction and was powering back toward us.

Orm's laugh cut off abruptly.

Dakkar moved past me, came alongside Orm's canoe, and grabbed hold of it.

"Get off!" bellowed Orm, and I let out my own laugh as I paddled harder.

"If the statue gets me, then we're both going under," I heard Dakkar say, a lilt to his easy tone.

I didn't watch to see if Orm snuffed out the balls of light that were drawing Skadi's fire. Instead, I drew my bow, and one by one, sank arrows into the two remaining targets.

CHAPTER 32

REYNA

The statue stilled instantly, and I heard clapping. Not a lot of clapping, but a smattering.

Then I heard a roar.

"You made her win!" Orm sounded furious.

I pulled myself from the canoe, tipping un-gracefully onto the marble stone on the other side of the fountain just as Orm leaped from his own canoe.

"The human girl won, Orm," called Kaldar as she squeezed water from her braids. "Deal with it."

The crowd were on their feet around us, and I could see Mazrith's huge dark form moving closer than everyone else.

"Listen to me, you cheating piece of horseshit," snarled Orm, turning to Dakkar and shoving him in the chest. "I don't know why you did that, but you'll regret it."

Dakkar tipped his head back and laughed, long and loud. "Cheating?" He tilted his head, fisting his hand on his hip. "You spent most of your time trying to get revenge on Lady Kaldar, instead of trying to win. You think that is an honorable way to play the game?"

"Silence! You—"

But Dakkar kept talking. "Orm, you underestimated the human, again. She beat you. And she will keep beating you. Do you know why?"

All the color had drained from Orm's face, but his neck was tinged with purple. Much as I was enjoying seeing Orm being ridiculed by the earth-fae, his fury had tipped to rage and I wasn't sure that was good. I could see his hands shaking around his staff.

I stepped backward, aware that Maz was close now, but unable to take my eyes from Dak and Orm.

"Enlighten me," hissed Orm.

Dakkar leaned forward, so that his face was right in front of the gold-fae's. "Because you have no honor. No valor. No courage. And she,"—he pointed at me—"is dripping with it."

A flash of light was the only thing I saw, but I heard the sickening crunch.

There was a shriek, and when the blinding light cleared my heart skipped a beat.

Dakkar was lying on the marble, blood pooling around the wound in his head.

The fierce slave girl he'd clubbed to death smashed into my mind and I stumbled backward, into Mazrith.

"Dak!" screamed Khadra's voice. "Dak, no, it can't—"

"You will die for this!" Henrik's roar reached me, rising over the other chatter of startled spectators.

Gold-fae guards descended on the charging earth-fae, Khadra screaming the entire time. Vines were snapping from her staff, lights flashing from the gold-fae trying to keep her and the others back. "Let me go! I have to get to my husband, let me go!"

"My Queen, this cannot be allowed!" bellowed Lady Kaldar over all of the noise, whirling to the Queen on her throne. "Lord Orm just killed in cold blood! He must be punished!" The Queen blinked in affable indifference. Her son stood from his throne, gripping his mother's arm. With a few words and a tug on her sleeve, she stood.

Everyone but the enraged earth-fae fell silent, staring at the Queen.

"Reyna Thorvald, of the Shadow Court, wins the game," she said with a smile.

Her eyes found the blood-soaked body of Lord Dakkar and there was a flicker of sharp focus in them. But then her son pulled her away, and it vanished.

"My Queen, this is not right!" yelled Kaldar. But the Queen and her son were moving, a ring of gold-fae guards closing in around them as they disappeared from view behind the dais.

Kaldar whirled on Orm, ten feet from where he stood. "All the champions knew the risks, but this!" She waved her arm at Dakkar. "This is not honorable, or part of a peaceful games festival! And her?" She pointed at where the Queen had just fled. "Tell me you are not behind making her so meek?"

The whole crowd were on their feet now, voices rising, confusion spreading, the screams and wails of Khadra ripping through the air, only Kaldar's amplified voice louder. Expressions were changing everywhere, tense alarm on the gold-fae faces, confused outrage on the visiting fae's.

Orm dragged his eyes from Dakkar's lifeless body, and his eyes instantly sought Queen Andask.

Mazrith gripped my shoulders, and his voice sounded in my head. "We leave, now."

"What about Dakkar? We can't leave him, or the others—"

"It is too late, Reyna. Look."

Queen Andask was nodding, her eyes alive as her shadow beast poured from the end of her staff. Her guards were closing around her, and I realized with a jolt that the gold-fae guards were creating a ring around the whole area.

"You are correct, Lady Kaldar!" Orm bellowed, making me jump. "The Queen is not herself. A small sickness, I think. And I'm afraid I can't do as you wish and tell you I am not the one responsible." A cruel smile twisted his lips. "I had not planned to do this so soon, but it appears that my hand has been forced."

Every shadow-fae standing with Queen Andask turned to us, and Orm's eyes fell on me.

"I wanted to see the *Leikmot* through, to earn my place as it's winner. But"—he cast his eyes at Dakkar's body—"I suppose that is not to be."

"What have you done to the Queen?" shouted Kaldar.

Orm glanced dismissively at the ice-fae. "She is weak, both physically and in will. Her son's greed was easy to take advantage of, and now she is paying the price." He shrugged. "Members of the Gold Court!" He swung his arms out, facing the crowd. "You must see this as a perfect chance for me to prove myself as a worthy replacement of our weak-minded Queen and her pliable son! They are clearly not fit to rule. I, on the other hand, have maneuvered our enemies into our grasp. I know what it takes to rule not just our court, but all of *Yggdrasil*! And I have the allies to achieve it."

His cold eyes gleamed as they found Queen Andask again, and her shadow beast hissed into the shocked silence.

"You think you can keep us all here?" Mazrith growled. I heard his voice in my head after he spoke, just two words. *"Get ready."*

"I think a few important hostages from the Ice Court and the Earth Court will further my cause, and I already have rooms picked out for you two in the palace." His voice had taken on a bitter snarl, and Mazrith hands were tight around my shoulders. "Yours, Shadow Prince, is in the dungeons, but yours, dear girl, is closer to my rooms." What I feared was lust filled his eyes, and he rasped the last few words. "Where my bound concubines belong."

"Now!" Mazrith bellowed. He must have spoken to the other fae in their heads, because they responded instantly.

With a roar, Khadra broke through the gold-fae guards, and a hail of vines and rocks smashed into the back of Orm's head, making him stumble. The rest of the earth-fae rushed in behind her, roaring and firing every magical missile they had.

"Ice-fae, attack!" yelled Kaldar, and ice shot from the staffs of every one of her courtiers, still spread throughout the crowd.

In seconds Maz had turned me on the spot, and then we were running, Khadra's grief-stricken screams ripping through the air when she reached her husband.

CHAPTER 33
REYNA

We burst past the guards as the fighting broke out around us, shadows tumbling from Mazrith's staff and sending distractions in every direction.

I didn't think I'd ever run so fast in my life.

We powered down the stone steps, others running too, and I didn't stop to take a breath until we skidded into our camp.

The others were all on their feet, the noises of fighting carrying from the palace grounds. Relief that they were all okay, and that there was no sign of Svangrior, made my pounding heart slow a little.

"What's happening?" Kara said, but Frima was already moving, gathering weapons.

"To the ship. Now."

Nobody argued, or hesitated.

Tait was the slowest, and in the end, Ellisar lifted the

241

man over his shoulder as we raced down the path and into the fog filled forest. It was hard to see the way, but I trusted Maz and followed in his footsteps as closely and as quickly as I could.

Mercifully, the plank was still down when we reached our boat on the shore and nobody even slowed as we all raced up it, onto the deck. Frima and Mazrith's shadows billowed from their staffs immediately, filling the sail and pushing us from the beach in an instant.

I bent over, gripping my knees and gasping for breath, trying to calm my racing heart as we cut through the water.

This was it.

The Queen and Orm had made their move.

I tried to force the image of Dakkar's body out of my mind, but Khadra's heartbroken wails filled my ears so completely it was impossible.

Gritting my teeth, still breathing hard, I went to Kara.

Panic filled her face, and she was panting as hard as I was. "What happened?"

"Orm killed Dakkar. Kaldar demanded justice from the gold Queen, but Orm is controlling her somehow."

Tait paled, Brynja sat down hard on a bench, and Lhoris growled in his throat. "Orm took control," he heaved through long breaths.

"Yes. And Queen Andask is standing with him. Combined, they are a massive threat to this world."

"You said Dakkar is dead?" Brynja asked, her face red from running and her eyes wild.

"Yes."

My throat closed, and I felt tears sting my eyes.

I'd liked Dakkar but... that wasn't what was causing the swell of fierce emotion.

Turning away from my friends, my feet carried me to Mazrith.

I found him at the back of the ship, behind the cabins, staring out behind the boat. He jolted as I gripped his arm, turning to me. "Reyna, I—"

Tears spilled from my eyes and he stopped speaking immediately, pulling me close to him. "What if it had been you? Did you hear her?" I cried. "Khadra just lost everything. Everything."

I had never had something to lose like I did now. All I could think about was the pain if I ever saw Maz like that. Dead and lifeless.

"I couldn't bear to lose you. I couldn't go on." Another sob wracked me, and Mazrith pulled me even tighter into him, his staff across my back. "I am here, Reyna. I will never leave you."

I pulled my face from his chest and looked up at him through hot tears.

"She would take you from me. The Queen. So would Orm. Worse, they could make me—"

Mazrith lifted his fingers to my lips. "Stop. I am here, right now. You feel me?"

I took a breath, pressing my face back to his chest. "Yes. I feel you."

"Now, look at me." I did, and he swiped a finger

across my wet cheek. "Dakkar will grace the halls of *Valhalla*, and Khadra will join him when she is ready. You and I are here, now. And we will reach the Shadow Court and defend ourselves. We will rally the fae and humans there, and we will hold our ground. We will fight, Reyna." His voice softened. "As we have fought for each other."

"I love you. I can't lose you."

"You will not." He bent, pressing his lips to mine gently. When he withdrew, a gold rune floated from his cheek.

My grief flipped to anger in a heartbeat.

"I hate this! Why can't I be close to you?!" I pulled away from him, kicking at the railing. "I hate that I'm hurting you, I hate that Dakkar is dead, and I hate Orm! I loathe him!" I had never considered myself capable of killing somebody, but right now... the rage that was filling me could easily become lethal, I was sure.

Mazrith's face was filled with emotion, but he made no move toward me. "Use the hate, Reyna. Use the love, use it all. We can win."

"And... If we don't?" I forced myself to meet his eyes. "Is there a plan if we don't?" I didn't want to think about losing. But, even less did I want to let Orm lay a finger on me. "I won't let Orm take me, Maz." My voice broke on his name, and I swallowed down my fear, my rage.

Mazrith swelled before me, his staff billowing shadows, his face as fierce as I had ever seen it. "That male shall never touch you, Reyna. Whatever it takes, I shall ensure it."

I needed no clarification, no elaboration.

We were bound, fused, connected by our souls.

I trusted him with my life, and as he stared at me, the fear lessened.

I could face the Queen. And I could face Orm. As long as Mazrith was by my side, I could face anything.

"I love you," I whispered.

"I love you, *ástin min*." He reached for my hand, running his fingers over my ring. "We must write our own ending, Reyna. I know the fates decided our path for us, but we are not at its end yet."

I clung to his fingers, letting my racing heart settle, the rage and grief I had let myself get swept up in calm.

He was right. We had been set on this path, but *we* chose where it ended. The stakes had been set, Orm and the Queen had made their move. But right now, we were ahead. We were together, and we had a plan.

Get to the Shadow Court and defend it.

Frima appeared, shadows still flowing from her staff into the sail, and she dipped her head in apology when she saw us. "I'm sorry, but you need to see this," she said. "It's Svangrior."

The warrior was on one of the beds in the cabin, apparently unconscious.

Mazrith kicked him hard in the shin. He didn't respond.

"What would he be doing here? Do you think he was trying to run?"

"This is poor choice of ship to flee in."

"What's wrong with him?"

"He's breathing," said Mazrith, leaning over him. "But unconscious."

Ellisar shouldered his way into the cabin. After a short inspection, he straightened. "I don't know what's wrong with him, but he doesn't seem like he's in any danger, or about to wake up."

A dark look crossed Mazrith's face. "Leave him in there and watch the door. When he wakes, we may get some answers."

We all fell into a tense silence as the ship powered through the mists.

It was clear what was at stake, and the tension was palpable, everybody checking behind us constantly for any sign of us being followed.

Orm and the Queen must know that Maz would return to the Shadow Court and try to hold it. It was his home, it was defensible, and he knew it well. But if they believed that his Court would snub him, or reject him, maybe they didn't think he was a threat. Maybe they wouldn't follow us.

The reality was, he could hold the palace a while

with his warriors, but he only had Frima with any magic now. Ellisar would fight to the death for him, I was sure, but I didn't know how long they would last against Orm's power and a crazy powerful Queen with a mist-staff.

I glanced down at the staff at my hip and took another swig from the whiskey bottle Brynja had found and passed around.

How do we make you work, Odin curse it?!

The fog had mostly cleared now, and I stood up, restless and agitated. Frima stood with me, staff in hand, her shadows still propelling the boat along at breakneck pace.

"You okay?"

I reached the railing and nodded at her. "Yes. I wish I could do more."

"I know you liked Dakkar. I'm sorry to hear what happened." I looked at her and she dropped my gaze a moment. "I don't suppose you saw what happened to Henrik?"

"I'm sorry, Frima. I didn't. The guards had him and he was fighting. Hard. But we ran before the fight fully started."

Emotion crossed her eyes before they hardened. "If he dies he shall grace the halls of *Valhalla* then," she said sternly.

"On Odin," I answered, the proper reply, before staring out at the still water.

Only, it wasn't still.

My stomach dropped as I saw a flicker of movement, then more as I swept my gaze up and down the more visible roots.

Eyes. There were eyes everywhere. And when I looked into them, hands and heads appeared over the edges. Hands and heads missing flesh, bits of bone and sinew showing.

My head swam and my blood turned to ice.

We were surrounded by Starved Ones.

CHAPTER 34

REYNA

"Maz!"

Frima and I called his name at the same time, as the Starved Ones began to pull themselves over the edge of the river, toward the boat.

"How far are we from the tree?" I asked, unable to tear my eyes from the approaching creatures.

"At least another hour." Shadows were already moving from the sail and powering into the creatures instead, forcing them back through the water.

Mazrith ran toward us, saw the Starved Ones, and moved to the railing on the opposite side of the boat, cursing.

Cabin doors opened and Kara, Lhoris, and Tait came out.

"What's happening? Have they caught up with us?"

Kara's face was fearful, then she saw what was in the water.

"Get back in the cabin and lock the doors!" called Frima.

My legs finally started working, and I moved to where I'd dropped my bow and quiver on the deck. I may not have useful magic, but I could shoot the bastards.

Ignoring everything else, I drew the bow and focused.

My first arrow found its mark, hitting a Starved One in its empty eye socket with enough force to smash it backward across the river, flailing.

Lhoris appeared beside me, a bag of throwing axes at his feet. He launched one with a roar at a creature that was mostly skeleton, and it shattered in the water.

I took aim and loosed again. Over and over, I released arrows at the undead creatures closing in on the boat, zoning out all the sounds and activity around me.

"Reyna, I think there is a problem," Voror's voice spoke into my mind, just as I loosed an arrow.

I cursed as it went wide. "Voror, don't distract me!"

"Turn around." His voice was alarmed enough that I did as he said. Kara and Tait were slumped on the planks in front of the cabin doors, as though they had fallen exactly where they had been standing.

Frima was leaning against the railings, trying to say something, but no words coming out. I watched in confused paralysis as her eyes closed and she slumped to the deck, Lhoris collapsing on my other side a beat later.

"Maz!" I ran to the other side of the boat where he and Ellisar had been holding back the creatures. The huge human was unconscious on the planks, and Mazrith spun to me.

The mottled patches on his skin were faintly visible, his scars standing out clear.

"What happened to them?" he barked.

"I don't know!" Panic was flooding me, and I knew my side of the boat was now unprotected.

"Reyna, keep shooting," he started, but his last word slurred.

"Maz?"

He dropped hard to one knee.

"No! No, no, no, what's happening?"

"Reyna," he tried to say, but on the last syllable he slumped forward.

I dropped beside him, rolling him over, trying to keep blind panic from consuming me. He was breathing, but unconscious.

I jumped up, racing to the other side of the boat. The Starved Ones had made ground in the respite from mine and Frima's defenses. I didn't have long.

Whirling on the spot, I tried to come up with any kind of plan.

A whimpering sound caught my attention, and I snapped my eyes to an open cabin door.

"Brynja?"

"I didn't know they would attack!"

"What?"

She stared at me a beat, then began to scream a name that almost made me stumble in confusion. "Rangvald!"

"What the fuck—"

But Rangvald ran from the cabin Svangrior was in, his staff out and shadows billowing from it. "Back, foul creatures!" he shouted, before running to the railings.

"Brynja, what—" I started, but Rangvald shrieked and I turned.

"Help me keep them back, help me!"

I stared at Brynja a second longer, my mind spinning, then ran to the other side, drawing my bow.

But it was too late. They were everywhere, and they were too close. I could see two, their slimy, rotten hands already pulling themselves up the shallow hull of the boat. I loosed arrows at both of them, but only hit one hard enough to dislodge it.

"Brynja, get everybody inside a cabin, now!" I yelled.

But when I glanced over my shoulder she hadn't moved. She was just staring, wide-eyed.

I ran to her, grabbing her shoulders. "I don't know what you've done but you need to snap out of it, now! Help me move them!"

I ran to Maz, grabbing his arms, trying to tug him away from the railings. "Brynja, Freya help me, I will hurt you if you don't start helping me!"

"I didn't know they would attack," she said again.

Rangvald shouted from the railings, and began backing up, toward the middle of the deck.

"In the cabin, my love!" he yelled at Brynja.

My love?

I tugged Mazrith again, but I couldn't move him, he was too heavy.

Hands appeared over the railing, followed by heads.

I was running out of time. "Brynja! Help me save them!"

But she had gone, she and Rangvald slamming the cabin door shut behind them.

I roared as I pulled, managing to slide Mazrith a few inches across the wood.

Was this how it ended? After everything? Mazrith and all my friends unconscious, only me awake to see us all pulled part by monsters, to be rebuilt as the undead?

Panic and bone-deep regret swamped me as the first creature pulled itself up and over the railings. I drew my bow, but my hands were shaking.

I stood over Maz, one leg either side of him, and tried to aim as the thing began to lumber toward me.

Just as I loosed, the whole boat heaved beneath my feet.

The Starved One stumbled but I kept my footing, jamming the toes of my boots under Mazrith's weight.

A *boom*, then the boat lurched again.

Almost in slow motion, I saw the side of the boat splinter, then wood and planks flew out in a massive explosion.

I ducked, throwing myself over Maz, then shadows were billowing over everything.

I screamed as they wrapped around me, lifting me

bodily from the deck. I groped for Maz, but he was being lifted too. I spun, kicking and flailing, trying to see what was happening, then stilled as I saw where I was being lifted to.

The Queen's ship was behind ours. Huge and black, with her standing at the prow, her staff raised and the tendrils of shadows reaching out, scooping up everyone from our boat as her canons destroyed it completely.

I slammed down onto the black planks of the Queen's ship, but I didn't notice the pain. I scrambled to my feet as a huge translucent shadowy dome appeared over the entire deck.

One by one, the others slammed onto the planks too, Rangvald scrabbling as the shadowy tendrils lowered him directly in front of the Queen.

Everyone was accounted for, and a tiny stab of relief hit me as I looked out through the shadowy barrier at what remained of our own ship. The Starved Ones were crawling all over it as it sank into the river.

My relief was short lived.

"So, you thought you could outrun us?" The Queen's singsong voice washed across the boat. "Let me deal with these vermin, and I shall finally have what I need from my wayward son!"

Brynja struggled to her feet on the planks beside me.

"It was you this whole time?" I groped for anything

to defend myself with, my fingers finding the staff at my belt.

But Brynja didn't move to attack, just glared at me. The fear that had overcome her when the Starved Ones attacked had fled, hard resolve now filling her eyes.

"You were working with Rangvald to kill me," I repeated. It wasn't a question. "Why?"

She sneered at me. "Because he's in love with you, and he wouldn't kill you himself."

My face screwed up. "Rangvald?"

"No you fucking *heimskr*, Lord Orm! He's obsessed with you, and I couldn't fucking stand it!"

I stared at her. "You were never from one of the coastal clans, were you? You were never taken in a raid."

"No. I worked in the palace, for Orm. And he sent me to the shadow court, as a thrall, to spy on the Queen."

"But Orm is working with the Queen. Why would he spy on her?"

Again, Brynja's face screwed up. "He's only working with her to get that infernal staff from her - he will soon get rid of her and make me his Queen."

I tried to piece the information together. I had been so convinced that whoever it was had to have magic, I hadn't even considered her. But she had been using Rangvald.

"Why Rangvald? Why didn't you or he tell the Queen about the shrine if you knew about it?"

"Yes, dear advisor, answer her!" bellowed the Queen, making us both jump.

Rangvald was kneeling on the planks, shaking. His face was as white as a sheet.

The shadows that had lifted me to the Queen's ship wrapped around my legs, forcing them to bend.

I fought, my face heating with the effort. Wasted effort. With a crack, my knees hit the planks.

The Queen's gaze was still fixed on Rangvald. "So?" she whispered. "My most trusted advisor? What do you have to say for yourself?"

Rangvald stared up at the Queen. He opened and closed his mouth, but nothing came out.

A Starved One threw itself against the shadowy dome but bounced off into the water.

The Queen raised her mist-staff, and the hideous shadow beast burst from it. Slowly, it prowled toward Rangvald.

"The *shadow-spinners*!" he spluttered, his voice desperate. "You had killed so many, and at first, when Brynja came to me and told me she knew what Prince Mazrith and the girl were up to, I thought they were finding a way to make new staffs! But when I discovered they were trying to find a mist-staff, I agreed to help Brynja kill the girl instead." His head dropped. "I am sorry, my Queen, I should have told you. I'm sorry, please. So, so sorry." He began sobbing.

"Why would you help her over me?" the Queen said, thoughtful a moment. Then her wild eyes snapped to Brynja. "Sex," she hissed. "You gave him your body in return for his magic."

"It was worth it. My true love will understand," Brynja said.

The Queen tipped her head back and laughed. "Your true love?"

"He only wants your staff, not you!" Brynja shouted.

The shadow beast turned to her.

"Shall we ask him?" the Queen said with a smile. "Orm, darling?"

Hatred filled me as Lord Orm stepped out of a cabin, and onto the deck. His gaze was hard and fixed on Brynja. "You tried to kill her?"

"You were blind to how dangerous she is!" Brynja said, her eyes now looking manic.

"I need her alive. You knew that," he hissed.

"And now you have her! I have drugged her whole guard and delivered her to you!"

"Drugged? What have you done to them!"

She must have drugged Svangrior and planted the bag in his tent too.

"Silence!" the Queen's voice was like a whip. "I have had enough of this." She banged her staff down on the deck, and with a silent, deadly leap, the shadow beast spun. It launched itself at Rangvald, and my stomach lurched as it ripped his head clean off. Blood covered the planks, and I closed my eyes, trying to keep from falling into total panic.

"I am here. I can't get through her shadow barrier, but I am beyond it." Voror's voice flowed into my mind, and I clung to it.

He was safe, and he was over the river. I wasn't alone. Not completely.

When I opened my eyes, Brynja was shaking, her eyes fixed on Rangvald's body.

Orm strode over to the Queen, and faced the hand-maid. "They are searching for a mist-staff?" he asked her.

She dragged her eyes from the headless corpse and looked at him. She nodded.

"And? Did they find it?"

"I—I-I think so," she nodded.

"Then why are they not defending themselves against these creatures? Why did they run when you killed that pathetic earth-fae?" The Queen directed the question at Orm, and light fired in his eyes.

"I think it is time we find out." He walked over to Mazrith.

"Get away from him!" I tried to get to my feet, but the shadows held me too tightly. "Get the fuck away from him!"

Orm wedged his boot under Maz's body and rolled him over, then looked at the Queen. "My love, can you read his mind when he is unconscious?"

"You know I can't, darling. I will have to wake him." The Queen snapped her eyes to Brynja. "What did you drug him with?"

Brynja mumbled a word I didn't recognize.

"Excellent. Finally, I will have your secrets, Prince Mazrith Andask."

CHAPTER 35

REYNA

The shadow beast vanished, and in its place appeared a huge sinewy paw, with claws the size of my hands. The clawed paw floated through the air, to Mazrith's head. The shadows swirled around him a moment, and he groaned.

"Maz!" His eyes didn't open, but he was making a faint noise. "Leave him alone!" I screamed, pulling as hard as I could against my shadowy restraints. But they were too strong.

The fact that she was able to use her magic like she was, while keeping the shadowy dome over the ship, was testament to the strength of her staff. I glared at it, willing it to explode in her face.

Maz groaned again, and his eyes flicked open.

"Maz, we're on the Queen's ship, she has us—" I started.

He burst to his feet in a whirl of action, his shadows blasting out at the shadow-paw as he roared.

A beam of light shot from Orm at the same time as the shadow dome over us flickered. One single Starved One's arm got through, and I realized with a jolt that they were crawling all over the shield now.

The Queen gave a bark of anger, and the Starved One was ejected forcefully from the dome. When the light Orm was projecting around Maz cleared, my heart stuttered in my chest.

Mazrith's staff was in pieces.

And he looked just as I had seen him in the vision.

The Queen's shadowy ribbons wrapped around him as he roared and fought, and Orm stared open mouthed at him. "What in the name of Odin are you?"

"I am done waiting to find out," snapped the Queen. The paw rushed Mazrith, the claws wrapping around his head, and Maz's cry was lost to the sound of my own screams as they sank into his skull.

A minute of complete torture passed, and I fought with everything I had to free myself and help the male I loved. I tried to force myself into her head, but with Voror outside the shadowy dome, my magic didn't respond to my desperate will.

The claws continued to dig through Mazrith's head, his face a mask of pain, and his lip bleeding as he bit down on it to stop himself screaming.

I had no such qualms about making a noise. I hurled every single curse I could possibly think of at the Queen and Orm, a torrent of unbridled, useless rage.

All those years with words as my only weapon - it was still the case. I was useless. Unable to defend those I loved. Anger consumed me, fear and rage making my insides burn.

The claws finally moved away, hovering in front of Maz, and he slumped forward, shadows keeping his arms bound behind his back.

"Maz!" Tears were streaming down my face. I couldn't watch her torture and kill him. I couldn't. I wouldn't.

"Interesting," said the Queen, her wild eyes alive as she turned to Orm. "I knew his mother had an affair, but I did not know that the Prince here was the result of that affair."

Orm's mouth fell open again, then his cruel eyes narrowed. "You mean..."

The Queen nodded. "Indeed. Prince Mazrith here is your brother."

Mazrith's head slowly lifted. "What did you just say?" His voice was a slur, and I found myself unable to add a thing, finally shocked into silence.

"I knew your mother was in love with a gold-fae, you stupid child," the Queen snapped at Maz. The black patches of skin swirled on Mazrith's skin, his eyes filling with black as he stared at the Queen. "And his pathetic wounded pride was what killed the king," she laughed. "Do you want to know what happened to the male everybody thought was your father?"

"As long as he is dead, I do not care," growled Mazrith.

Orm held his hand up. "Wait, I need to ask — you are utterly repulsive!" His lip curled as he looked down at Mazrith. "What *are* you?"

"Darling, allow me to explain," said the Queen in her sing-song tone. She ran a tongue over her black teeth, her eyes gleaming. "Mazrith's mother had an affair with a gold-fae — your father. When she birthed a gold-fae child, the king realized he was not the sire and tried to force his own magic into the boy. This is the result." She waved her staff at Mazrith, and my rage burned so hot I thought it might melt my skin.

The Queen turned back to Maz. "Once I was married to the king, I made it my business to find out who your mother had been visiting in the Gold Court. Rumors of her infidelity were sparse, but I have a way of getting information from folk. Somehow, your mother managed to ensure that nobody knew you were illegitimate, as I'm quite sure my subjects told me everything they knew." Madness sparked in her eyes as she referenced those she had tortured over the years. "I needed leverage to get the king's staff from him. And that's how I met Orm." She beamed at the gold-fae. "It was *his* father your mother had been in love with. I told the king that I knew who the gold-fae who had taken his wife had been. I told him that he should go and kill him, to restore his pride." She laughed. "Orm was waiting for him."

Mazrith blinked at Orm. "You killed the King of the Shadow Court, while he wielded a mist-staff? How?"

Orm shrugged. "An ambush. It was simple really. He snuck into our rooms, killed my father, and I buried a knife in his back while he was relishing his victory. He didn't even know I was there."

"Then my sweet Lord brought me your father's staff. I told everyone he had handed it over to me while he searched for the vanished gods, and Orm and I bided our time until we could rule both courts together," the Queen said sweetly. "I thought removing you would be my hardest obstacle, but look at you! You are not even a shadow-fae! You are no threat to me or my Court, *at all*."

The unhinged look took her face again. "You know, I could make folk believe I did this to you, and use you as a model of what I will do to those who disobey me." She cocked her head. "I might remove a few limbs though. Orm, darling, let me keep him?"

"Of course, my love."

Her tinkling laugh was interrupted, and I snapped my head to Brynja in surprise.

"He doesn't love you." Her face was white, and her body was trembling, but her voice was loud and clear as she repeated the words. "He doesn't love you!"

The Queen's face twisted. "Don't be so ridiculous,

you can't possibly think that he is in love with a pathetic creature like you?"

The girl tried to straighten. "Look inside my head. See the nights we've spent together, the things I have let him do to me." She swallowed hard. "I belong to him."

Fury washed over the Queen's features. "I shall remove those memories form your head forever, you maggot!"

She advanced on Brynja and the girl threw her arm out, pointing at me. "It's her he wants!" She half-shrieked the words. "He's obsessed with her!"

The Queen paused, flicking her black eyes to me. "My darling," she purred, her eyes on me, but her words for Orm.

"Lies and nonsense, obviously," the gold-fae said.

"You saved her life in the Ice Court! You talk about her in your sleep!" Brynja choked.

The Queen turned slowly to Orm. "The weaselly girl makes a point. Why did you save her life?"

"I needed her alive," Orm growled.

The Queen tilted her head. "Why?"

"Revenge," he said, stamping his foot. "That disgusting creature and she have made a mockery of me with their binding. She was supposed to be *my* bound concubine!"

"You still wish her to be your concubine?" The Queen's tone had turned dangerous.

Would they turn on each other? Could I use it to my advantage if they did?

"I wish to seek revenge," said Orm, answering the Queen, his voice a hiss. "I thought you understood revenge. It is one of the things I love most about you," he said, switching abruptly to charm.

"Lies!" screamed Brynja. "He doesn't love you! He doesn't love *me*! He loves her!" She pointed wildly at me again, and the Queen whirled to face her.

"Enough!" With a snap of her staff, shadows lifted Brynja from the planks, whooshing her to the top of the dome. "You are no longer welcome on my ship," the Queen snarled. A gap opened in the dome, and she cast the screaming girl out into the clawing hands of the Starved Ones.

Bile rushed my throat, and I forced my eyes away just in time to see the gleam in Lord Orm's eyes as he stepped into the Queen's back. Light flared around him, and the Queen jerked hard, her eyes expanding so wide I saw white around them for the first time.

"She's right. I don't love you," he hissed in the Queen's ear. "And it's remarkably easy to take a mist-staff from those who aren't expecting an attack."

He shoved her and she stumbled to the planks, a dagger jutting out of her back.

Her mist-staff clattered on the wood, and for the briefest second, time froze, everyone staring at the staff.

Mazrith and Orm lunged at the same time, and I stared in horror as the dome over us began to disintegrate.

CHAPTER 36

REYNA

Orm reached the staff first, bellowing his triumph.

"Put the shield back up!" I screamed, running toward Mazrith. Orm's face warped as he looked up, the shadow now so thin it was barely holding up the weight of the undead.

He held out the staff, but nothing happened.

Mazrith was struggling to his feet, stumbling, and he pointed at the Queen. "She's not dead. The staff won't respond to anyone but her while she lives!"

"Can you make a shield?" I asked desperately, but I already knew the answer. He had no magic — his staff had been destroyed.

"Work, curse you!" yelled Orm as the dome failed, and Starved Ones fell to the deck.

Mazrith threw a fist at the first one that landed near us, and I swiped desperately with my useless staff.

I had magic now, but it would do nothing— what could I achieve by getting in anyone's head?

Panic speared me as more creatures swarmed the boat, moving toward the still lifeless forms of my friends, piled where the Queen had dumped them in the middle of the deck.

Orm bent, shoving the Queen's body toward three creatures advancing on him, and I almost heaved as one yanked her arm clean off her body and a gurgling sound came from her throat, barely audible over the noise the creatures were making.

She wasn't dead yet, and they were pulling her apart.

The many, many she had tortured flashed through my mind, and then something grabbed my shoulder and wiped her clear from my focus. I smashed my staff over my shoulder, connecting with something behind me. Maz bodily threw a mangled, rotten creature away from us, a bite leaking dark blood from his forearm.

"Stand back to back with me!" he yelled, and I moved, almost numb with fear.

Shadows flurried and I snapped my head up to see Svangrior, awake and firing fierce whips of shadows at every creature coming near him or the pile of unconscious bodies by him.

"That is enough, my petals," sang a voice, and my insides turned to ice. "We have what we came for, and no harm must come to her. Yet."

The Starved Ones all fell still, their too-long arms

and awkward gaits freezing as the Elder climbed over the railings of the ship.

"Reyna Thorvald. It is time to meet your fate."

"Take me, leave the others," I said, feeling dizzy as I stepped away from Mazrith.

With a roar, he moved back in front of me, raising his fists. "Touch her and die," he snarled, and for a beat, he was a terrifying as the undead.

"Maz, look at me!"

My churning thoughts had slowed eerily, and in the stillness that had followed the attack, clarity had seeped in.

Mazrith's black eyes were filled with golden swirls as he whirled to face me, huge and hulking. I laid my arm on his shoulder.

"I can't run from this," I told him. "I've run my whole life, and there's nowhere left to go. It's me she wants, and she won't stop until she gets me. And I would never forgive myself if anyone else was hurt. That includes you."

He snarled, half-feral. "I will never leave you. I told you that."

He turned back to the Elder. "Both of us! You can take both of us without a fight if you spare the others."

The Elder grinned her hideous grin. "You are not in a

position to bargain, silly little children." She gestured behind us. "Open the gates."

I turned, seeing the tree of life looming, the Gold Court doors before us.

Orm hurried to the front of the ship, raising his staff, his face a mask.

"No, you can't let them in there!" I said, as Mazrith barked,

"Do not let them inside the sacred tree!"

But Orm had already sent his light to the two braziers on either side of the gates, and they began to swing open.

The ship moved through easily, and the Elder limped toward the Queen.

"This one lives, barely," she said, then flicked her wrist. Two of the creatures gave hideous wails, then set upon the Queen.

I forced my eyes away, fixing them on the Elder.

"What do you want with me?"

She tilted her head. "Can you really not know?" Her eyes moved to my staff. "Why does it look like this? This is not how it looked before."

I looked between her and the staff as the doors closed behind us.

Yggdrasil reacted instantly. Darkness spread over the bark, a cloud of blood-red dust descending over the towering statues, and all the light and green and sparkle of the place receded. The black, blood-covered planks of the ship seemed even darker.

"You've seen this staff before?" I asked, forcing my attention back to the Elder and trying desperately to ignore the sounds of the Queen's body being pulled apart.

She took another limping step toward me, and the smell overwhelmed me.

I gasped, stumbling backward, and she snarled, her grin still fixed. "Undo what was done! You are the only one who can. If you refuse, I will make you one of us."

"Undo what? I have no idea what you are talking about!"

"Then they die."

Starved Ones dragged Svangrior, kicking and cursing, and the other unconscious members of our group into a line. "Choose which one dies first, child," the Elder sang.

A Starved One who was mostly bone, thin strips of flesh hanging from one half of his ribs, hauled Frima's body up and over his arm.

"Stop! Show me! Show me what it is you want me to do!"

The Elder turned back to me. "Show you?"

I nodded, and before she could say another word, I did the one thing that scared me more than anything else in the world.

I entered her mind.

. . .

Everything spun, and the hunger was debilitating. Overpowering. All consuming. There was nothing but the next meal, the taste of flesh, the warm blood —

"What are you doing?"

She was talking. To me.

"Show me why you need me!"

"Get out!"

With a force that felt like I'd been smashed in the head, I was ejected from her mind. I tripped and went sprawling, right at her feet. Maz growled and sprang, and the Elder reached down, closing her bony, rotten fingers around my wrist.

Everything went dark, and then I wasn't on the boat inside the tree anymore.

I was in a forest, on the edge of a small town. A woman with long copper hair was surrounded by men, all shouting and jeering at her. Tears streaked her cheeks, but her expression was fierce and hard.

"I will not do it!" she shouted, banging a staff on the ground.

"Then he dies!" roared a man waving an axe in the air, scores of braids in his brown hair.

They were human, all of them, and they parted to let a cart roll in front of the woman. A man was tied to it, rags stuffed into his mouth.

"No! Let him go!"

"It's an abomination, you two together. Fae and humans have no business being married!"

"Let my husband go, now!" the woman said, light starting to sparkle around the top of her staff.

"Do as we ask, and he lives," growled a woman, holding a dagger to the man's throat. She pushed, and blood welled up as the man coughed around his gag, eyes wild.

"Please, stop! You can't make me do this! You should win a war with valor and honor! Not by forcing me to make them all lose their minds!"

"The Scyfling clan deserve to lose their minds! And besides, what point is there having a fae in our village if we can't make use of her?" a man jeered. "You are a rune-marked fae, you can fuck with their minds until they are all gibbering wrecks. Fates, you could even make them think they were animals!"

A roar of cruel laughter went up from the group.

"If you don't send them all mad, your daughter will be next. And trust me, they have much, much better uses for her than slitting her throat," the woman said. When the fae did not respond the woman shrugged. "Then see that we are serious. You are responsible for his death." She thrust the dagger into the man's neck.

The fae female screamed, dropping to her knees, and the man with all the braids gripped her by the neck, pulling her back up.

"Do it, now. Or your daughter becomes our play-thing, and so do you."

She sobbed and held up her staff. "I'm sorry, Harald.

I'm so, so sorry," she cried. But the tears were made of light, and when she straightened, rage, rather than grief shone in her face. "May the gods burn you all," she hissed.

"The gods don't burn folk like us," the man leered. "That's reserved for you fae."

"So be it," she said, her eyes filling with solid white. The staff exploded with light, and when it cleared, the humans around her were in pieces. Flesh hung from shattered bones, blood everywhere.

But still they stood.

"What...what have you done?" The woman who had held the dagger choked around the missing half of her jaw.

"What you asked me to do to your enemy," the fae said. Her eyes were still white, her voice carrying a power that would bring the strongest men I knew to their knees. "You took what I loved from me. And I have taken everything that made you human." The staff continued to glow, brighter and brighter, and then a voice boomed through the sky.

"The rune-marked serve the Vanir, and you have used their magic without permission. You go too far, Estrid."

The woman threw her head back and called out to the sky. "I regret nothing! Punish me as you like, but these humans shall be human no more!" There was a flash of green light, and she was gone.

The vision lifted, and I stared at the Elder, still gripping my wrist.

"A rune-marked fae created the Starved Ones," I breathed. "Using this mist-staff to steal Vanir magic."

"You *mother* created us," the Elder hissed. "With that staff. And only you can undo what she did."

CHAPTER 37

REYNA

The Elder released her grip on me. "Free us."

"Free you?" I continued to stare at the staff, the vision whirring through my head, everything spinning.

They had killed my mom's human husband to try to force her to harm other humans? And she had taken rage-fueled revenge and cursed them instead.

I looked up at the statue of the Vanir High Priestess Maz had pointed out all that time ago.

How do I use this staff? I projected the question at the statue, and the staff flared hot in my hand.

Darkness descended once again, and when it lifted, the vision was like nothing I had been given before.

A voice sang out, female and lilting.

"These futures three are meant for thee. Choose your path: honor or wrath."

Images began to flash before my eyes.

In the first, I saw myself holding the staff high like my mother had, light dancing around it. But I was using it to free the Starved Ones. As soon as I did, the staff itself turned to mist, dissolving in my hands, never to be used again.

In the second, the Starved Ones lived, and I used to staff to control them. They ringed the Shadow Court palace, where I ruled with Mazrith by my side, the creatures keeping all who had ever hurt me or dared to oppose me cowering in fear.

In the third, I saw myself on the Gold Court throne. Except it was no longer the Gold Court. I had used the staff to destroy the Starved Ones, not set them free. It would be centuries before they reformed. And I had used it to destroy the gold-fae. Every one of them. All those who had scared, taunted, abused or hounded me. They were all dead, and the staff lay across my lap as I sat on my glittering throne.

I opened my eyes.

Mazrith was staring at me, as was the Elder.

I stepped away from them both, clutching the wooden staff, still hot in my hands.

"If I use this to free you, then I lose it. All its power. Mazrith will lose his Court, never wield his magic again."

The Elder took a step toward me, and Maz shook his head. "I don't want power. Just you."

"Or, I could use this to control you," I said, and the Elder paused. "I could use this to turn you into my weapon." Mazrith's swirling eyes widened. "Reyna, why would you—"

"Or I could use it to destroy you."

She had been the woman in the vision with the dagger, I was sure of it. The one who had killed my mother's husband. My father?

"You were turned into this because you were murderers and rapists."

I looked around at the devastation on the deck of the ship, the two creatures putting the bits of body left of the Queen back together, Orm cowering at the prow. "And you, you are just as cruel, just as deserving of their fate," I cried at the gold-fae. Rage was building inside me, and every time I cast my eyes near Maz, it worsened, knowing what he had lived through. "The gold-fae are fucked-up, cruel, honorless creatures who are trying to change this world into their own twisted playground. They are no better than the Starved Ones were when my mother cursed them!"

"Reyna," Maz said, holding his hands out, his voice calm. "*I'm* a gold-fae. Evil is found in individuals everywhere. You know this."

I looked at him, my head beginning to pound. "Orm killed Dakkar, he killed the warrior woman." My words were tumbling, my mind spinning. Heat was surging from the staff into my body, turning me about inside, confusing me.

Voror's voice sliced through the chaos. "Orm is evil.

All gold-fae are not. The Queen was evil. All shadow-fae are not."

"And the Starved Ones? You believe they deserve freedom?" I half shouted the words.

"We have paid the price," said the Elder.

"If that were true the gods would have saved you. But they didn't, they left you here, like this, because you deserved it!"

"They left them here, like this, to test us," said Mazrith. "You know what the right thing to do is, Reyna. You told me to choose honor."

"And look what they did to you!" Tears ran down my face as I stared at him. "It's not fair!"

"Remember what we said, Reyna. We must write our own ending. You choose who you want to be."

"I say you destroy them." Orm's voice made me turn. The Elder hissed, and two creatures lunged for him.

Instinctively, I raised the staff. A single crystal burst to life at the top, and the creatures froze.

Panic filled the Elder's eyes.

Slowly, Orm lifted the Queen's mist-staff. *The now very dead Queen.* "I never thought to own two mist-staffs, but one that controls an army of undead?" He smiled and flicked his staff. A swirling ball of light flew at the unconscious bodies of my friends.

I moved my own staff, but all it did was make the Starved Ones cry out.

Mazrith launched himself in front of the ball of light, and gut deep fear swamped me.

If it hit him, he would die.

I threw my consciousness inside his head, taking control of his body as though it were my own.

Power flooded me, and I rolled his shoulder, forcing him out of the way of the ball, and lifting the staff at the same time. A confused Starved One shrieked as I launched it into the air, directly into the ball's path.

Mazrith slammed into the planks. The Starved One exploded.

"Reyna!" He choked, but my gaze was locked on Orm, and I lifted my staff as he lifted his.

The second I'd seen Mazrith throw himself in front of my friends, my decision had been made.

I held the staff high and screamed at the Vanir statue.

Swirling shadows and gloom descended on the boat. I dropped to my knees and crawled to Maz, tears flooding from my eyes as the Starved Ones wailed.

"Where's the staff?" Maz choked as I reached him.

"Are you alright?"

"Yes." He rolled, coughing, grabbing for me as the gloom began to whip into a tornado of red light and the screaming got louder. "Where is the staff? What did you do?"

I held my empty hand out. It had, just as the vision had shown me, turned to mist.

"You freed them."

Before I could answer, the Elder screamed. Her rotten fingers closed over Orm's arm, and he cried out, lashing at her. "You would seek to control us?" she hissed, then clamped her half-missing jaw onto his neck, tearing a chunk away. Orm's eyes flashed a moment, then he slumped as blood poured from the wound.

There was a thunderous clap, and everything stilled. The dark shadows disappeared in a puff, and sparkling copper light filled the air like fairy dust.

The Starved Ones all began to rise into the air, screeching and flailing.

"What have you done?" screamed the Elder. With a jerk, she was lifted from her feet, dragging Orm's limp body with her.

Her form began to flicker and flash, and I gasped as I realized it was happening to them all. Human forms appeared over their monstrous ones for a split second.

I forced my eyes back to the Elder, twenty feet above the deck. An expression of peace settled over her face, and then they all vanished, the tiny copper sparkles falling to the deck like rain.

We stared, dumbstruck, as Orm's staff clattered to the planks, the gold-fae vanished with the undead.

CHAPTER 38

REYNA

S ilence blew through the tree, the light and life
and color returning.

"What in the name of all the gods just
happened?" murmured Svangrior.

With a rush that brought fresh tears to my eyes, I
launched myself at Mazrith. "I'm sorry. I'm so sorry I
didn't keep the staff and that I can't give you your magic
back." The tears kept coming, as though not crying for a
decade had all been in preparation for falling in love.

Mazrith pushed me back, gripping my jaw, his eyes
swirling with gold and black, just like the ring on my
finger. "The Queen is dead. Orm is dead. Our enemies
and those who would seek to destroy what is good in
Yggdrasil are gone." He bowed his head, pushing his
hands through my hair, away from my wet cheeks. "All
because of you," he whispered.

"But I—" He planted a kiss on my lips, stopping me from speaking.

"You did exactly the right thing. You showed the valor and honor that you made me see was worth living for."

"You're sure?" I whispered. Emotion was tearing through me, a whirl of adrenaline and energy, and all laced with regret. "You found me to help save you."

He shook his head, cupping my face. "No, *ástin min*. I found you because I loved you. Because I was destined to find you."

Voror swooped down, landing on the planks beside me. "Reyna, I believe there are answers here, inside *Yggdrasil*. We should seek them."

I looked down at the owl, still clinging to Mazrith's arms. "Now?" I whispered.

"Now."

He took off, flying toward the ring of statues, and I saw a flowing pull of copper sparkles swirling through the air, dancing around the Vanir high priestess.

I looked back at Mazrith. His scars were puckering, gold and black churning between the split flesh. He smiled, wiping the tears from my cheeks and giving me a gentle push. "Go. Trust the owl." He dropped his voice low. "He helped me say goodbye to my mother. He has friends in high places."

I stood up on my tiptoes and kissed him. "I'll be right back."

Moving to the railings, I eased myself over the edge

of the boat, lowered myself into the water, and gently kicked my way to the ring of statues.

I pulled myself up onto the cold marble toes of the Vanir high priestess and pressed both hands to the stone. Voror swooped down beside me, landing gently.

The marble heated under my hands, and I felt that surge of power inside me again. I poured my will into the stone, willing the statue to show me what I wanted to know.

And she did.

I saw a shadow-fae, standing behind who I now knew was my mother. Flashes of scores of images whizzed through my mind, enough to make me realize that the shadow-fae was my mother's handmaid. They were close. Friends.

I saw my mother's marriage to my human father, the disdain and torment they got from his village. Worse was the reaction my mother got from the other fae. They didn't throw stones or fruit at them in the street like the humans did, but they shunned her.

Over time, her bitterness grew. I saw her patience wear thin, only her love for my father making her happy. I saw my arrival in the world, and for a few years, she was no longer bitter. No longer resentful.

But then I was shunned. We couldn't live with the fae, not with a human in our family, so we lived with his clan. But they bullied me, tormented me. Held me under-water, pulled and cut my hair.

My mother performed tasks for the humans, usually

under duress, alongside performing her rune-marked duties for fae of all magics. I saw her arguing with my father. She told him we were not safe, even with the powerful staff the Vanir had blessed her with. He told her that her power was too strong to let any harm come to her family, that she should believe in herself.

It is humans I do not believe in, she said, as he walked away.

War broke out with a rival clan, and she became fearful. She returned to our home, with ten-year-old me in tow, and my father was gone, the interior destroyed.

She and the shadow-fae handmaid fled to a forest, and she hid me inside a tree. I cried and cried, and then she held up her staff, and performed an enchantment. I fell asleep, and she sobbed as she gave her instructions to the handmaid.

If I am not able to return and wake her, you must hide my staff, and leave a trail — one only she will be able to follow. She will be able to wield my staff, she will be able to see what to do. I have disguised her as human. Wake her when the time is right. Cheeks wet with tears, she straightened to her full height. *Now, I find my husband.*

I knew what happened next. I had already seen it.

They killed her husband, and the Vanir took her.

But this time, I saw the shadow-fae handmaid too. She retrieved the staff and returned to the Shadow Court, where she hid it inside the mountain, then pledged her service to Mazrith's mother.

A flash showed the shrine as a dusty cavern, the

female burying the staff in the dirt. As soon as she left, the statues formed, the stone arm bursting from the dirt, the chasm forming beneath it.

The gods? Or the Vanir? I didn't know.

Decades later, when Mazrith was born and his mother mentioned that he was dreaming of a copper-haired female, the handmaid realized the time had come. She returned to where the staff was hidden, and discovered the ring of statues, and no staff. Not knowing what else to do, she wrote the inscription on the palm, and told Mazrith's mother.

She found the tree I had been hidden in, and as she touched me, I awoke. Seeing my gold rune-mark, she took me to the Gold Court palace. She died, trying to get back to the Shadow Court.

The world flashed before my eyes again, and then I was seeing green everywhere.

A forest, thick with life.

A female, so bright with shining light I could barely make her out, was speaking with an owl.

The owl blinked, then vanished.

Suddenly, information began filling my mind — words, histories, and memories that were not mine flooding me, making me gasp.

The female held up a staff, and the light around her dimmed. Under the light, her hair was shining copper. She turned with a smile, looked straight at me, and then the vision ended.

. . .

My cheeks were wet again as I drew in long breaths, pressing my forehead to the stone statue, soaking up all the knowledge that had just been poured into my head.

My mother had sent Voror, from the Vanir home-world, high in the canopy above *Yggdrasil*.

I was the only rune-marked fae left in *Yggdrasil* because my mother's actions had changed everything. The Vanir decided there was too much power wielded by the rune-marked fae, and that the balance of humans and fae was wrong. They made the rune-marked human, and removed their history from the scriptures. But I was protected by my mother's magic, inside the tree.

I belonged nowhere; I could live wherever I liked.

I could be whoever I wanted to be.

And I knew exactly where that was.

I stood, shaking. I went to speak aloud to Voror, and stopped, realizing I didn't need to.

Voror? I projected the words silently, straight to owl, and he fluttered his wings.

Yes.

Did you see all that too?

No. But I got an impression. I am from the Vanir homeworld.

Yes. And, I hate to tell you this, but you're stuck with me. We're...

I searched for the right word.

Bound, he said.

Yes. Bound.

He sighed into my mind, then fluttered his wings. *There will need to be some changes to the way we live.*

I smiled, then lowered myself back into the water.

I had a feeling there were about to be a lot of changes to the way we lived.

CHAPTER 39

REYNA

Mazrith leaned over, pulling me from the water with ease when I got back to the boat and passing me furs to dry myself with.

"The others are starting to wake up," he said quietly. "Svangrior took them all inside the cabins while he dealt with the bodies."

I cast an uneasy glance across the deck and saw that the blood and fallout was mostly gone.

"Is everyone okay?"

He gave me a smile. "They are fine — they were asleep. Nothing wrong with anyone. They are all in the dining cabin now, raiding the Queen's supplies."

"How did Brynja drug you all?"

Maz shrugged, his chalky skin catching the warm light. "The whiskey she passed around."

"But I drank that too."

"She must have given you something different. And

288

she tricked Svangrior. She told him I had asked him to meet me on the boat. Rangvald was waiting for him. He ambushed him, then drugged him."

I let out a long sigh. "All that time. We could have just looked in her head at any point and found our traitor."

Mazrith stepped toward me, taking my hand. "You are safe now. Was Voror right? Did you get answers?" He gestured at the statue.

"Yes. I have so much to tell you."

"Good. But, before you do..." He held out his other hand, and I stared down at what he was holding.

"The Queen's mist-staff?"

"I know a rune-marked or two that could refashion it," he smiled at me. "Take it. It's yours, by right."

I shook my head. "No. I don't want it."

"You're a fae," he smiled at me. "You can wield that better than I ever could."

"No," I said. "I don't need a staff for magic, and I don't need any more power than I already have." I pushed his outstretched hand back at him. "Tait can remove the stain the Queen has left on this, right? He can turn it into something new, something right for you?"

Mazrith paused, and I thought he would argue. But before he could, the staff top disintegrated, leaving nothing but a simple rod of wood. He looked at me, frustration in his eyes. "It seems I turn all powerful staffs useless," he snarled.

I frowned, then realized with a start that I could see

movement in the air, copper dust sparkling and flowing around the staff. *Around Mazrith and the staff.*

"I'm not so sure," I whispered. "Maz, do you want to become a shadow-fae?"

He raised his eyebrows at me. "Yes."

"You're sure?"

"The Shadow Court is my home, and I wish to rule there. And..." He dropped my gaze, flicking it to the staff, then back. "And I will miss my mother's magic. Shadows are a part of me now. Or, they were."

I smiled at him, nodding. "Maz, do something for me? Keep something of the real you. This you that you have been forced to hide your whole life."

"*Ástin mín*, I would do anything you ask of me, but this mist-staff is nothing but a lump of wood." He frowned, gesturing it at me. A burst of copper sparkles flowed from it, invisible to him, but dancing like a thousand promises before my eyes. "And besides, it was never able to change me before."

My eyes shone as I reached out and wrapped my hand around his. "You didn't have me before."

Shadows exploded from the end of the staff, whirling and pouring around Mazrith, the copper sparkles flitting and swirling amongst them.

When the rush of power ebbed, I let go and stepped back, letting the shadows flurry to a stop.

When they cleared, Mazrith was standing tall, the end of the mist-staff now a solid gold raven, with a black snake winding around it.

"It accepted me. It *wanted* me," he said on a whisper. "It's beautiful." But I was staring, transfixed at him.

"*You're* beautiful," I gasped. And fates above, he was.

The chalky white skin and the scars were gone, his usual smooth, tanned skin returned. But the black mottled patches had stayed, now swirling with gold, just like my ring.

Gold streaked his black hair, and whirled through his irises too, and I felt like he was bigger, taller. Stronger.

He beamed at me, lifting his staff, and when the ribbon of shadows burst from it, they too had streaks of gold running through them, shining. "*Ástin mín*, I think you used your gold-giving on my staff," he whispered, then glanced down at his bare forearms. "*On me.*"

We are bound, I told him, delighting in the shock on his face when I projected the words directly into his head. *The Vanir statue showed me how to use my magic.*

"What else can you do?"

I shrugged, then stepped in close to him, winding my hands up his neck and into his hair. "I don't know yet. But I can't wait to find out," I grinned, before pressing my lips to his.

CHAPTER 40

REYNA

"**M**az! You're not supposed to be here!"

I wrapped a huge sheet around myself as he stepped into our bedroom.

He grinned at me, casting his eyes lingeringly over my sheet-wrapped body. "I know. But, I have a gift for you."

"A gift? If you are referring to your—"

He stepped into me, cutting me off by pressing his lips to mine. "No," he whispered against my mouth, and I wished that *was* the gift.

I accidentally sent him an image of us on the bed, and he growled. "Okay, I take it back." His hand moved to his belt "That *is* my gift."

I planted my hands on his chest and pushed him back. "Kara and Frima will be here to help me get ready any minute," I forced out, my cheeks heating.

"Then, I want to give you this before they get here."

His golden-black eyes shone, and my heart swelled just looking at him.

He was truly something unique. Something special.

And in a few hours, he would be my husband.

He pulled a compacted wooden staff from his waist, and held it out to me.

"Tait worked with Lhoris to make it, but they wanted me to give it to you."

I looked between him and the staff. "Really?"

"Tait has been living in the library since we got back, trying to find out what kind of staff a rune-marked fae might have."

"It's not that I'm not grateful, I am truly touched," I said, looking at him. "But I don't need a staff."

He smirked at me. "Really? So you don't think it might help you control the images you keep flinging into people's minds? Or help you stop plucking things from theirs that you don't want?"

I blushed deeper.

He was right. I had been having some control problems. "You think it'll help?"

"Yes. Your mother had a staff for a reason."

"My mother had a mist-staff and was so powerful with it she sent me to sleep for centuries and created a race of monsters," I muttered.

Maz chuckled. "Take it."

I reached for it, and my mouth fell open when I saw the top.

It was an owl, made of clear crystal, tiny specks of

293

copper throughout it, shining and dancing in the firelight.

"Oh fates, it's beautiful," I breathed. I willed myself to connect with it, and almost stumbled, my sheet slipping as I caught myself.

"Woah. The power..."

Mazrith's eyes had darkened as he stared at me. "You are naked and projecting power like a fucking beacon. No force on *Yggdrasil* is going to stop me from throwing you on that bed and taking you right now," he growled.

There was a knock at the door before I could tell him to go ahead. "Reyna, I have your dress and wine. Lots of wine," called Frima.

Mazrith's chest rumbled as I scooped up the sheet, my face hot and my cheeks stuck in a huge smile. "Except the force that is Frima."

He gave my now-covered chest a regretful look, then wound an arm around me, kissing me.

"Thank you for the staff, Maz. It's amazing."

"Thank Lhoris and Tait when you see them." He reluctantly let me go. "I'll see you soon, my Queen."

Frima really had brought a lot of wine.

"So, Frima got a letter from Henrik today," Kara said, swinging her legs over the side of the bed as Frima tried and failed to do something with my hair.

"You know, Brynja may have been a traitorous piece

of horseshit, but she really was good at your hair," she muttered.

I snorted, looking at her in the mirror. "What did Henrik say?"

She glanced at me. "They held a memorial for Dakkar."

Sadness swept over me. "And Khadra?"

"He hasn't seen her since. Nobody has."

I sighed. "I hope she's okay."

Frima gave me a look that clearly showed how naive she thought I was, then smiled. "The Gold Court Queen has stepped down, made her son the ruler."

"Really? He's a child!"

"True, but he's smart, and by all accounts, nowhere near as vain or likely to succumb to flattery as his mother. She's embarrassed by how easily Orm got to her and her family. Her Court lost faith in her, so she didn't have much choice."

"I hope Maz likes the new King," I said. "His mother always wanted the Courts to work together."

"Well, there is a *Leikmot* to finish," Frima grinned at me. "I hear they're good for fostering trade relations."

"Ohh no," I said, shaking my head. "If there are to be any more games festivals, I am not taking part."

"Well, you are technically the strongest fae in *Yggdrasil*," said Kara mildly.

I gave her an alarmed look. "Of a Court that doesn't exist," I said. "There is no-one for me to represent."

295

"You're about to become the Queen of the Shadow Court."

"No, no, no. I will be the wife of the King of the Shadow Court," I said quickly. "The Shadow Bound Queen," I added, using Lhoris' words. *Mazrith's* Queen. "That is not the same."

We fell silent, until Kara spoke again. "Do you think you'll ever meet the Vanir?"

"No." I had seen enough from the statue to know that the high fae would never come down from their home in the canopy of the great tree of life. They served the gods, away from the fae and humans. And I was a one-off. I knew that. And in some ways that felt absolutely right. The scope for the abuse of my power... It made me shudder to think what Orm or the Queen might have done with it.

I turned around and smiled at Kara. "I don't need to. I have a family, and they are all right here."

She beamed, and Frima rolled her eyes. "When you came here, you were not so soft."

"When I came here, I was a kidnapped thrall," I retorted, then lifted my wine glass.

"From slave to Queen," Frima said, lifting her glass too.

Kara joined, and we clinked the glasses together.

To love, I added in my head.

CHAPTER 41
MAZRITH

I strode along the corridors, my amulets clinking around my neck.

"You're not nervous, are you?" Ellisar said, banging me on the shoulder.

"No. I am keen to see this through," I said, eyeing the now navy walls, inlaid with golden snakes.

Svangrior snorted. "You are the one who should be nervous," he said.

Ellisar actually blushed, worry filling his large brown eyes. "You think she will say yes, right?"

Svangrior rolled his eyes. "Yes, you *heimskr*. Kara goes gooey-eyed every time you talk to her. She'll say yes." Relief flooded Ellisar's face. "Odin only knows why though, you're a fucking—"

I stopped listening to them, concentrating on my own worries.

The truth was, I was nervous.

Not of being wed to Reyna. As far as I was concerned, the two of us had been as good as wed since she told me she loved me in the forest.

But I needed my court to accept her. I needed the world to see that we were together, and I knew she hated being paraded in front of the fae like this.

She had assured me that a formal, royal wedding was fine, and that she understood its importance.

And I believed her. Mostly.

The throne room had been changed, since my return to the Shadow Court. As in the room my stepmother had used had been sealed, and an entirely different wing of the palace had been given to receiving courtiers.

Navy walls were covered in both silver and gold scrollwork, statues of ravens, owls, and serpents placed along the long carpet leading to the thrones.

The windows at the end had been left clear, on Reyna's request.

To let the starlight in. The view is too incredible to hide.

Odin's raven, I loved her. She had made me what I was, literally.

Guests stood as I walked in, my fur cloak draping behind me, the crown on my head proud.

I disguised the deep breath I took as I smiled at my guests.

The courtiers I knew had always been loyal, and the staff who had served my palace so loyally.

I had barely reached the end when the harp in the corner burst to life, and Voror swooped through the open doors to the throne room.

My breath caught as Reyna appeared, holding Lhoris's arm.

The guests all bowed their heads as she moved up the carpet, Frima and Kara behind her.

I noticed none of it.

All I could see was her.

The dress was the same black one she had worn to the ball, but it had been altered. A high, regal neckline had been covered in golden chains and glittering crystals, and the golden bottom of the dress had also been adorned with sparkling clear gems. A train had been added, shining and catching the light.

But no part of the dress shone as brightly as her. All my worry that she did not want to go through with such an event fled.

I could see how much she wanted this. Wanted me.

On cue, an image burst into her mind. Me and her, holding hands and kissing as the binding took place.

I smiled as she reached me, immediately taking her outstretched fingers.

"You look stunning."

"So do you," she whispered.

Svangrior stepped up between us, and the guests all took a seat.

I scanned their faces. All I could sense was wide-eyed admiration.

"We are here to seal the betrothal binding created between Prince Mazrith Andask and Reyna Thorvald."

Reyna beamed at me, and I squeezed her hand tight.

"Hold up your wrists," he said, and we both did, along with our staffs. Reyna's new crystal owl glinted in the light, my black raven rippled with magic.

"Do you accept each other for all of eternity?"

"For all of eternity," we both said, and magic flowed from the staffs, winding around our interlocked hands, then down our arms.

When the whisps faded, the bound mark was hot and bright on my wrist. Black, laced with gold. I looked at Reyna's, then at her face, just as she stepped into me.

"I love you."

"And I love you."

I kissed her, and when I pulled back, she stared up into my eyes. *We chose our own path.*

We always will.

Her face changed suddenly, alarm crossing her features.

"What is it?" I asked her aloud.

Emotions flowed into me. Her feelings.

Life. There was a stirring of life... *inside her belly.*

My heart stuttered in my chest. "Reyna..."

Her face lit up with the truest, most beautiful smile I had ever seen. Every fear, every doubt, everything that wasn't her beaming at me, melted away.

"I have found my family, Maz," she said, her eyes filling with tears. "And I will never run again."

THE END

Read on for the author's note of thanks, and the first few chapters of Lucifer's Curse.

THANKS FOR READING!

Thank you so, so much for coming on Mazrith and Reyna's journey with me.

This series has been so incredibly enjoyable to write. I have not written in a Norse mythology world before, so the research involved was a joy, but I also have not written a cast or plot this complicated in a while, and I loved it.

I know this series has taken me longer to get out than my previous ones - that is partly because of the sheer amount of plotting and research required for the size of story, but also because of some life stuff! I am just so grateful you've been patient and stayed with these characters. They have truly stolen my heart.

I went darker with Mazrith's backstory than I had intended to, but it didn't feel like I had any choice. He is who he is because of what happened to him, and I became a little obsessed with his journey. I love him, so much! And Reyna is everything they both need her to be. Giver her a weapon, and she'll take no shit! She spent her life running from something she couldn't escape. She represents facing your fears for me, and how what is showing on the outside does not always match what is happening on the inside.

I could not have written this series over the last year without the constant support I have around me. My husband (who has still not read any of my books but confidently assures me I'm good at what I do, haha), my mum, and my author friends (

Simone and Sacha especially) are all so important to me, and I'm beyond grateful. THANK YOU.

And thank you to my editor, who doesn't just make the sentences better, she makes my plots stronger. And deals with my shocking inability to do what I say I will, when I will.

MOST OF ALL, THANK YOU LOVELY READER!!

Seriously. I do this full time, and I can keep doing it because you keep reading. I love you.

Eliza xxxx

Oh, and I had another pic of them getting it on done! This one is a little more risque than the last one. (You see him. All of him. If you know what I mean.) You can sign up at elizaraine.com!

Printed in Great Britain
by Amazon